MW01519418

Scary Short Stories

Jordan Grupe

Manor House

No Sleep Tonight / Jordan Grupe

Library and Archives Canada
Cataloguing in Publication

Title: No sleep tonight : scary short stories / Jordan Grupe.

Names: Grupe, Jordan, author.

Identifiers: Canadiana 2021016283X |

ISBN 9781988058689 (softcover) |

ISBN 9781988058696 (hardcover)

Classification: LCC PS8613.R88 N6 2021 | DDC C813/.6—dc23

Note: This collection of short stories is a work of fiction. Any resemblance to locations or persons alive or dead is purely coincidental.

Front Cover art: Adam Laws / Shutterstock / (Silhouette of Cathedral in Hamilton, ON at sunset)
Back Cover art: Ryan Davie (photo of Author)

First Edition
Cover Design-layout / Interior- layout: Michael Davie
240 pages / 54,785 words. All rights reserved.
Published 2021 / Copyright 2021
Manor House Publishing Inc.
452 Cottingham Crescent, Ancaster, ON, L9G 3V6
www.manor-house-publishing.com (905) 648-4797

Funded by the Government of Canada | Canadä

For Vanessa
Thank you for everything.
Love you, mom.
P.S. Feel free to skip the gory bits.

Acknowledgements

First, my thanks to you the reader - this book wouldn't be possible without you.

Many thanks as well to my mom, Vanessa. You are a constant inspiration to me. Your kindness and generosity do not go unnoticed by me or the rest of the world. I'm in awe of you. Thank you again for your endless encouragement, and so much more.

Thank you to my wife, Chloe. You help me to look at the world in a different lens and you make me a better person. You inspire me every day. I love you so much.

Sincere thanks to Mike Davie and Manor House for publishing this book and my debut novel *Beneath the Asylum,* fulfilling a lifelong dream of seeing my work in print - I really can't thank you enough for taking a chance on this upstart Internet writer. Thanks also to Ryan Davie and the rest of the family. I love you all.

Thanks also to Nolan, my brother. When I write you're almost always my imaginary reader. You did what all good older brothers do, you showed me the good shit. Kurt Vonnegut, Joe Hill, Nick Cutter, etc. Thanks for having great taste. Hope you liked this one too. Thank you to all my friends and family as well for supporting me in my writing. I love you all.

Finally, a word of credit to someone whose story on a podcast inspired the premise of "I spent a week on the ocean floor... I'll never step foot in the sea again." My thanks to Garrett Reisman, an astronaut and diver, who actually did spend a week on the ocean floor.

- **Jordan Grupe**

Table of Contents:

About the Author – 7

I Won a Cursed Lottery – 9

The Garden Gnomes are multiplying – 25

I spent a week on the ocean floor... I'll never step foot in the sea again – 39

I now know why no one sleeps in Room 14 – 47

I visited an abandoned penitentiary – 53

We were told not to break Quarantine – 65

I Thought my pet squirrel caught the Bubonic Plague – Now I realize it's something far worse – 87

I fell down a bottomless pit – but that wasn't the worst part – 95

I'm trapped in my new VR horror creation – 121

We stumbled upon a serial killer while camping – 133

This is not a healing pool – 143

I'm pretty sure my barber is a serial killer – 155

My wife has an ugly side when she sleepwalks – 161

Mr. Gleam – 173

I met my doppelganger – 181

My cat and I joined a neighbourhood social club – 189

Don't get off until the door is open all the way – 197

General Reed's worst day – 205

A Tale from the Tower – 217

Added Bonus: A Taste of Jordan's next book – 229

Praise for *No Sleep Tonight...*

"Despite being a relatively new addition to the horror writing scene, Jordan Grupe has made a name for himself as an excellent storyteller. His ability to build characters and terrify readers is consistently impressive as he continues to produce high quality horror content. I have featured a few of his tales on my YouTube channel "Mr. Creeps" and the response has always been amazing!"

- **Mr. Creeps** (683,000-subscribers on YouTube)

"Jordan has a knack for making the mundane menacing (I'll never look at garden gnomes the same way again). His stories are immersive, dragging the reader in kicking and screaming, with just enough humor to help wash down the absolute dread you experience when visiting his wicked worlds."

- **Travis Brown** (Grand_Theft_Motto on Rededit No Sleep), author, *House with One Hundred Doors*

"From **Jordan Grupe**, author of the gripping and terrifying novel *Beneath the Asylum,* comes the appropriately named *No Sleep Tonight* collection of scary short stories – the latest offering of terror for those yearning for a bout of wild-eyed insomnia."

- **Michael B. Davie**, author, *The Late Man*

About the Author:

Jordan Grupe is a Hamilton, Ontario-based author and artist, who has created more than 40 short stories, novelettes, and novellas.

His writings are often shared with a vast audience in the hundreds of thousands via the websites Reddit.com (under profile Jgrupe) and YouTube as well as author website: JordanGrupe.com.

The author and his works are also featured on an array of other websites, including amazon.com and other Amazon sites; the websites of other major books retailers and the publisher's website:

www.manor-house-publishing.com.

Beneath the Asylum was his first novel and it drew its inspiration from the author's own experience as a security guard at a psychiatric hospital with a dilapidated, and reportedly haunted, old mansion on its grounds.

No Sleep Tonight continues the author's tales of horror with his first collection of truly scary short stories.

No Sleep Tonight / Jordan Grupe

I won a cursed lottery

From the moment I bought the lottery ticket it didn't feel right. I never spent money on lottery tickets, and thought they were a waste of money. But a sign on the street corner caught my eye when I was walking home from work one day.

Community Lottery:
Money raised goes to a good cause –
Current Jackpot $2,234,423

I was intrigued for some reason. It was a lot of money and I didn't imagine a lot of people were playing, since it looked like a small operation.

I went inside and a small old man with a fine moustache stood behind the counter. The store looked a little rough inside - the paint was peeling from the walls and the shelves were half-bare. It smelled a bit like mildew and spoiled meat.

The shopkeeper smiled at me warmly as I walked up to the counter, the light dancing in his eyes behind his round spectacles. He wore a distinctive black suit with gold cuffs and collar.

"Welcome, welcome, what can I do for you?" He said in a friendly tone.

9

"I saw your sign outside and wanted to buy a few tickets for the lottery," I said.

"Of course, of course. All money raised goes to a good cause. Two dollars for one, five dollars for three, ten dollars gets you seven tickets. How many you want?"

He was pulling out a crisp stack of tickets, their faces appeared to have been inked by hand. But that wasn't possible considering the size of the jackpot, I thought, they had to have been stamped. Yet each one looked different. They weren't numbered. They looked like Rorschach tests, each one a unique black blotch of ink.

I was feeling lucky. I told him I would take as many as fifty dollars would get me. There wasn't a price break past ten dollars so I ended up with 35 tickets. I flipped through them, amazed at how different they each were.

"Good luck – remember all money raised goes to a good cause." The man's face was bemused, his mouth turned up at the corners into a little smile.

"Anything I should know? How do I find out if I won?" I asked the man. His brow wrinkled, his face looked annoyed by this question. "I've never played this lottery before, it seems a bit strange."

"Someone will tell you if you win, don't worry," he said cryptically.

I didn't understand how they would find me, but he refused to take any of my information. I left the store feeling like I had been ripped off. Fifty dollars for a handful of black and white tickets with cool designs on them didn't seem like a very good deal. I was experiencing buyer's remorse for the first time in years as I walked home. I was usually very frugal. I couldn't help but wonder what had gotten into me.

A week later someone came to my door. It was another old man wearing the same black suit trimmed with gold as the shopkeeper. He was holding a ticket with a black abstract pattern on it, like a Rorschach test. He didn't say a word, just held up the piece of paper and stood there, smiling. The black splotch looked like a devious little monkey, and I recognized it immediately.

I ran upstairs, excited, and grabbed the stack of tickets. I shuffled through them and found one that matched. I made a high-pitched yell of excitement. I was rich! I waved the ticket with the monkey ink-splotch on it above my head and danced. I couldn't believe it – I'd never won anything before in my life.

I brought the whole stack of tickets down with me just in case but kept the monkey one separate. I showed it to him and he smiled, nodding his head. He took out a check from his pocket and handed it to me with a flourish, then began to walk away. It was a check for twenty two hundred dollars.

Furious, I tried to contain my anger. I ran in front of the man and cut off his hasty escape. He looked surprised. I told him the sign had said the prize was over two million dollars.

"Two thousand two hundred dollars was a long way away from that," I added

"Money goes to a good cause. You are not a good cause. You take twenty two hundred dollars and be happy," the man said.

I couldn't believe my ears. His smile had faded and he looked very serious now, as if I had broken some unspoken contract. I thought of a 50/50 draw at a stag and doe or at charity events where the winner was expected to donate their winnings to the cause. Was that what this was? I thought of the man's words: *All money raised goes to a good cause.* I hadn't even bothered to ask the name of the charity.

"Listen, if you try to screw me here I will come after you guys for false advertising. I see what you're trying to pull. I won this thing fair and square - now give me what's mine," I told him, gritting my teeth.

I had never been a greedy person, but the idea of two million dollars that was rightfully mine being taken from me rubbed me the wrong way and brought out a very bad side of me.

I had already mentally begun to spend the money and felt robbed and cheated.

If I wanted to give some of it to their charity that was my decision to make, a greedy and unfamiliar little monster's voice said inside my head.

He furrowed his brow. His eyes looked sad for a second, but he reached into his pocket and pulled out another check. He put the other one away and handed me this new one instead. The amount written on it was *$2,234,423.*

I jumped up and down, giddy with delight. When I opened my eyes again, the man was gone. I couldn't believe my luck. I had thought I would only get half that amount, at the very most, after some negotiating.

No one contacted me to ask if I wanted to have my picture taken with a big cardboard check, and I was a bit disappointed, but I decided I wouldn't let it bother me. I had over two-million dollars to spend on whatever I wanted. No one called to ask me to donate a portion of it to the organization's charitable cause, but I just assumed they would send something by mail.

First things first, I thought, and called my job. I quit without notice, playing punk rock on my laptop as I did so, and singing "Take this job and shove it," out loud as the hold music played in my ear. I sang the lyrics to my manager, letting him know "I ain't working here no more!"

My boss was furious, but I just hung up on him. "Holiday in Cambodia" came on the playlist next and I listened to the furiously jovial tones of Jello Biafra with a big smile on my face as I lay on the couch.

It felt good to be in charge of my own destiny for once, or so I thought.

I went to the bank to deposit the check. After talking to managers for a while they made a phone call and confirmed the check was real (probably should have checked that first before quitting, haha). They told me it would take a little while to clear, so I would have to wait a week or two to spend any money.

I sat around my apartment for a couple weeks playing video games, watching old movies, and enjoying the unemployed lifestyles of the soon-to-be rich and famous. Finally the bank called and said I could play with my cash. The manager tried to tell me something else but I hung up on him before he could waste any more of my time. The guy's voice was dry and boring and suddenly I had no attention span for boring. After a lifetime of normality I was ready to have some fun.

I went to the BMW dealership first. I had always wanted one and decided I would treat myself to an M5. They obliged and I burnt rubber out of the car lot watching their surprised faces as I drove away.

The car had a lot of torque and was tough to control due to my lack of experience with high performance vehicles. I didn't let that bother me, though, and gunned it down main roads until the cops pulled me over and gave me a hefty speeding ticket.

The price of the ticket didn't bother me, but the points against my license did. I already had a couple of recent speeding tickets from prior infractions and the cop told me with this most recent mistake I would need to go in front of a judge to plead my case regarding why I should be allowed to keep my license.

I bit my tongue and tried not to scream at him. My license would be revoked for up to six months if the judge decided I didn't need it that bad and/or wasn't remorseful enough. I tried not to worry about it too much, but two weeks later my license was revoked. The judge hadn't liked my attitude, apparently.

To get the bad taste of that experience out of my mouth, I contacted a real estate agent. I was in the market for a house, I told her. Something big, with a pool, the greedy little voice inside me said.

She showed me a few options and I settled on the nicest one of the bunch. It cost a cool million but it was worth it. I spent another day shopping and filled the house with top of the line electronics and comfortable leather furniture, a pool table, a Pac-man vintage tabletop game, and outfitted the back deck with a gigantic Weber Barbeque with a buttload of BTUs.

After all that shopping, I gave some money to friends and family who began to hound me for cash to help them pay down debts and to replace aging and broken-down vehicles. They had always been good to me, so I felt guilty saying no. I had some student loan debt so I wiped that out with a sigh of relief as well.

I had a terrible feeling when I logged onto my bank account and realized how much I had spent. I knew I was no longer a millionaire, but was surprised to see the balance was $655,573.24. I had spent two thirds of the money in three weeks. But at least I had a sweet ride and a great house to show for it, I thought.

I made a mental tally of all the things I had purchased and tried to make myself feel better but couldn't. I felt empty and hollow inside, suddenly. I couldn't understand the feeling, and tried desperately to get rid of it.

I took a trip to Hawaii. I got sick the day I arrived with a virus the doctors couldn't figure out. My travel insurance covered the hospital bills, for the most part. But the vacation was a bust. I came home a month later after spending all that time in the hospital. I hadn't even been to a beach while I was on my trip – I was so sick I couldn't spend more than ten minutes out of bed. Wounds and bedsores developed all over me, and my skin became paper-thin from the steroids the doctors prescribed to try to fight the illness.

I got a cut on my foot the day I got home and it stubbornly refused to heal. It wouldn't even stop bleeding and quickly became infected. I ended up in the hospital again, this time in an isolation room as my wound picked up another infection, nosocomial and resistant to antibiotics. Perfect, I thought. Just one more thing. What else could go wrong.

I started to regret not just keeping the check for $2,200. I was beginning to get the feeling my life perhaps would have been better if I had. This all felt like a punishment. The greedy voice inside told me I was wrong, but I didn't trust it.

My friends and family abandoned me and stopped visiting. I had become stingy with my remaining money and they resented me for it. They said I had changed, that I was greedy and indifferent to them. All I wanted was to keep some of the wealth as a nest egg, I told them. Was that so bad?

I was finally discharged from the hospital for the second time. I had lost 70 pounds and was emaciated and weak. I could barely walk and just getting out of bed exhausted me.

When I got home, I tried to enjoy my big house, but it was too large to get around, now that I was deconditioned from my long hospital stay. I had to get a nurse and a personal support worker to help me bathe and do housework. I had no strength left suddenly and felt used up and hopeless. I was afraid to look at my bank account now – the money in there was no good – it was toxic.

One night lying in bed, restless as I wriggled and squirmed trying to find a way to ignore the pain from the bed sore on my coccyx, I decided I should give the money back. Something told me that was the only way to fix things.

I sold the house and brought the BMW back to the dealership. After selling everything else of value, I ended up with around 1.8 million dollars back in my bank account. I felt like I needed to return the rest as well, but was in no state to do any physical labour in order to make money. It would probably take twenty years to save up the amount I needed to pay it all back, I thought. I prayed the men in black and gold would forgive me and return my life to normal somehow.

I called each member of my family and told them more or less what I planned to do – fudging the details only slightly.

I said I planned to give all the money to charity. I thought they'd be angry, but everyone told me I was making the right decision. They said the money had changed me, and certainly not for the better.

I made my way back to the little shop the next morning with the help of my PSW. He drove me there and helped me inside in my wheelchair.

The man at the counter was not the same and my heart dropped immediately. He was dressed in a white T-shirt that said "Florida" on it and blue jeans. He spoke in a twangy southern drawl and when I asked about the lottery he said he had no clue what I was talking about.

"We got all kindsa' scratchers, if that's what you're after," he said, pulling out the scratch-and-win tickets from beneath the plastic countertop. I shook my head and thanked him for his time.

We left the shop and I realized I had no clue what to do next. I knew I had to give the money back but how would I find the men in the black suits with gold trim?

I stopped a woman walking by and asked if she knew the people who owned the shop before, the ones who ran the community lottery. The woman shrugged and said she had lived there years but had never heard of such a thing.

I looked around and saw the street looked worse than it had the day I bought the ticket, a couple months before. The people looked sadder, the buildings were dirtier and looked in disrepair. Cars on the street belched thick grey smoke and rattled over potholes. Homeless people clustered on a corner where a little shanty was erected. Abandoned storefront windows were smashed, left un-repaired, the broken glass still laying scattered on the sidewalk.

I went home, anxious and upset. I needed to find the men in black suits with gold trim. It was the only way to get my life back, I thought.

In my motel room that night, I lay in bed, cold and scared. It didn't seem to matter how many blankets I put on I could never seem to stay warm. I had never put back on any of the weight I had lost, in fact lost more every week. I couldn't keep food down and had never-ending nausea. I thought I had cancer but all the tests came back negative at the hospital when I was there. Still, it felt like something horrible was festering and growing inside of me. The greedy little monster voice was always there, in my head, but I now ignored him and his awful desires. Still, he whispered to me constantly.

"The greedy thing inside you will eat you up," a voice said from the shadows in the corner of my dark room. The clock on my bedside table said 3:23 AM.

I tried to call for help but my voice came out as a strangled whisper. I tried to scream but no sound came out.

The light danced in the eyes of the man in the shadows, although there was no light in the room to be reflected. I saw him step forward out of the darkness. His smile was bemused, still barely visible.

"You should have kept your winnings when they were offered," he said.

"I'm sorry," I managed, tears steaming down my face. "What can I do? I want to give it back! Let me give it back!"

"You have all of it?" he asked, with a sly and knowing look in his eyes that said he knew I didn't.

"I tried.. but I have most of it. Over one million eight hundred thousand. I.. please.. Take it back. I don't want it," my words sounded pathetic to my own ears but I didn't care. I only hoped he would accept. He didn't.

"You must give it all back. The hoard must be whole to tip back the scales so they rest even once again," he said.

"How? Just tell me what to do and I'll do it!" I pleaded with him desperately.

"There are many ways to make a dollar. Find one of them. Then do it again and again until it's whole again." His face looked a little gleeful. The bastard was enjoying this.

"I can't. Don't you understand? It's impossible! I'll die before I can make ten dollars!" I was angry but tried to plead once more with him.

"There must be some other way, please. I'll do anything. Anything," my voice came out a whisper.

"Well," the man said, playing with the corners of his fine mustache, "you have one other option, although you may not like it..."

The next day I went to the address where the man had told me to go. I walked in and they gave me a hospital gown, although this was no hospital. I was directed to lie flat on a cold steel table, and told the doctor would be in shortly.

The man who came in was wearing black scrubs with gold trim. He introduced himself as Doctor Gold.

An assistant came in next, an older woman in glasses, dressed the same. She said her name was Nurse Black. They told me what would be done, and I said that would be fine. Whatever I had to do to get my life back, I would do it. They explained they no longer had an anesthesiologist, he had paid his debt. So I would be awake for the procedure.

They scrubbed large swaths of my body with a disinfectant that turned my skin pink. Then they began to cut.

The scalpel left a red trail of blossoming blood wherever it went, and soon the stuff was everywhere. Nurse Black mopped it up calmly with clean towels, wiping the sweat from Doctor Gold's brow every so often.

I screamed and wept. I gnashed my teeth and pounded my fists into the hard steel table as they reached into my body, severing arteries and veins, and pulling out slippery blood-soaked organs, which shone like rubies in the bright light of the overhead lamp.

I passed out after they cut off a portion of my lung, when I felt like I could suddenly no longer breathe. The doctor looked around with wide eyes for a moment, as if he'd made a bad mistake. I woke up once more and wished I hadn't. What I saw should not have been seen.

The price of my organs on the black market didn't quite cover the cost of my mistakes, Doctor Gold said as my eyes fluttered open. His words were fading in and out. I nodded my head when he asked me a question, though I didn't understand it. He handed me a pen and I took it in my shaking hand. I remember signing something, but didn't read what it said.

I wish I could tell you things worked out for me. I really do. And maybe they will someday. I only wish they'd told me what a crappy rate people pay for black market organs. I would rather have had my kidney and my left eye than twenty thousand dollars wiped from my debt. I have to pay the rest back in labor anyways.

At least they pulled that little monster out of me, kicking and screaming. A tiny, inky black monkey, made of greed and hate, screeching and howling as it dug its claws into my belly in a futile effort to stay inside me – to destroy me. That s the last thing I saw before the world went dark.

Maybe one day I'll get to work behind a counter somewhere, selling tickets. But for now I'm only tasked with inking them. Each blotch of ink has to be distinctive and different. And there are thousands, millions of tickets to make.

They don't give us breaks, either We live at our desks, receiving whips to the back from a cat o' nine tails when we fall asleep or slow down. They have IVs hanging from the ceiling, full of vitamins and amphetamines, which infuse into us all day long as we hunch over our desks.

I'm told the cost of the fluids and amphetamines are added to our debt every day, that it just keeps growing and growing. But that's just a rumor, no one gets to see their balance. People disappear sometimes and we hope they paid their debt and didn't just die of exhaustion.

I look ahead and see rows of people, puttering away at their desks, fading into the distance. This warehouse, or whatever it is, it's enormous. There are thousands of us here. All dressed in black with gold cuffs and collars.

No Sleep Tonight / Jordan Grupe

The garden gnomes are multiplying

My great aunt's obsession with garden gnomes was a bit of a running joke in our family. We would tease her about them at family gatherings, joking that they were taking over her property. She had more than a dozen of them scattered all over her back and front yard as well as in the garden.

So when she asked if I could drive her to the flea market one Saturday, I already knew what she was aiming to buy.

"Looking for another jewel for your front yard?" I asked, smiling. In my family we were always ribbing one another.

"Of course! There's a perfect spot by the front door now, since we removed that shrub last week. I need to get a special little guy to go there They'd better have something interesting."

When we arrived at the flea market, I saw they did indeed have something interesting. It was in the front window of the shop staring at us when we parked and my great aunt lit up with a big smile. I couldn't understand her reaction, since my first thought was that the thing looked malicious and cruel.

25

"There it is! That's the one!" She exclaimed. So much for shopping around.

She jumped out of the car while it was still rolling, dashing inside quickly on her arthritic little legs. I hurriedly finished parking the car and chased after her, stealing a backwards glance at the creepy little gnome. It was dressed in green and purple and had an evil grin on its small bearded face. It was holding an axe which glinted like a real blade in the sunlight.

"Excellent craftsmanship," the flea market owner was already saying when I got inside. He was walking back to the counter holding the thing carefully in his hands and I shuddered. The idea of touching it revolted me for some reason. He set it down gently on the counter and my great aunt began to fawn over it, preening its beard and running her finger down the long blade of the axe.

"Careful!" I shouted, a little louder than I had intended. They both paused and looked at me with their eyebrows raised.

"It's not a real axe blade, Jayson. Don't be silly," my great aunt said, rolling her eyes and turning her attention back to the man behind the counter. I saw she was right. The blade had looked real in the window but that had been a trick of the light, I surmised.

"How much?" she asked, opening her purse.

"This is a Von Welken original," the man said. "They don't come cheap. He did all the detail work and painting himself, by hand. This was one of the last pieces he did before starting to pump them out like crazy last year. All the fine handiwork he was known for – out the window. It's sad he passed away last month. This one went up for auction at his estate sale, actually."

The man sure seemed to know a lot about gnomes, I thought. But my great aunt was nodding along as if she knew this already.

"Of course! It was so sad what happened to him. I've always wanted one of his pieces. Not the newer ones of course, but one of these with all the detail! It's stunning."

I had to admit, she was right. The gnome looked real. The fact that it was carved out of wood and painted by hand only made it more amazing. The features on the face were lifelike as was the rest of it. The clothing appeared hand-sewn and had little scuffs and rips in it, but of course it was all just a masterfully painted block of wood. The beard and hat had texture and definition to them, with just the right look of weight and feel. As someone who had dabbled in art and was a student of it all my life, I couldn't help being impressed by the sculptor's work.

The man quoted a price so high I actually laughed out loud. My aunt turned around and shot daggers at me. She didn't even haggle, just began pulling crisp fifties and hundreds out of her wallet and stacking them neatly on the counter. I couldn't believe my eyes. The revolting little thing was worth a small fortune. I tried to talk her out of it quietly but it was hopeless. She was angry that I would even suggest she pass on such an opportunity. This was an investment.

We got back to her house and she set the gnome down with great care in the spot she had planned for it. It rested evenly on the stump from the shrub which had been removed, looking very gnome-like on its naturalistic platform. She admired it for a moment, then shot me another dirty look and walked inside, slamming the door behind her.

I stood there looking at the hideous little gnome. The axe blade seemed to glint again in the sunlight, as if it had changed magically into real metal again. Out of the corner of my eye I thought I saw the little bastard wink at me. I shook my head and rubbed my eyes unbelievingly. There was no way that had just happened, I thought. I was just working too many night shifts.

I spent a bit more time there that day and managed to obtain my great aunt's forgiveness for my transgressions. She showed mercy and provided me with popsicles and cool lemonade, grateful for my assistance on such a hot day. I had to apologize for embarrassing her at the flea market, even though I was still disturbed by the gnome.

I did some research when I got home and found a bit of information online about the suspicious death of Mr. Von Welken. It turned out he had gone somewhat mad in the weeks and months before his death. He had claimed that it wasn't him making the myriad of gnomes in his workshop. The police had found quite an odd scene when they arrived at his suicide. I read on, fascinated.

*

My great aunt called me the next morning, hysterical. She wouldn't say what had happened on the phone, only that I needed to get over there right away. She said she was calling the police when she finished talking to me, and hung up.

I rushed over and arrived to find her pacing in the driveway. The police hadn't arrived yet, and I quickly found out why not.

"Someone destroyed my babies!" She was wailing as I pulled up in my car. She was still in her bathrobe, and complaining that the police were taking their time getting there. Didn't they realize this was an emergency?

I surveyed the damage. All the gnomes throughout the front yard and in the garden had been smashed to pieces. Actually, I realized, they looked like they had been hacked to pieces by the blade of a very small axe.

The backyard was the same. All of her gnomes had been destroyed, and small piles of wood scraps were left where they had stood the night before. All of the gnomes were obliterated. The one by the front door, though, was still there. Its tiny face smiled up at me, eyes full of mischief. The axe blade looked like it had little splinters of wood all over it, but that wasn't possible. I dismissed such a notion as pure insanity. Those were the kind of thoughts that got you locked up in padded rooms, I mused to myself.

But it sure did look like little bits of wood on the blade of the axe, like splinters from chopping up a bunch of other rival gnomes, perhaps? No, those were not the thoughts of a sane person.

I consoled my great aunt as she began to cry. I hugged her and she wept against my shoulder.

"At least I still have Mr. Winkles," she sobbed. Oh no, I thought, she's named the bastard. Mr. Winkles, what a name. I thought about his sly wink at me and shuddered. She went over to her one remaining gnome and picked it up, rocking it and smoothing down its wooden beard hair as if it had hairs askew. It was unsettling to watch.

I saw the neighbour's cat was trying to get into the house and I went up to the porch to give it a few pats on the head. My great aunt saw it too and set down the gnome quickly, hurrying after me. She loved the neighbour's cat, Lucy. It was practically hers, since she fed it every morning and evening, and it spent most days inside her house or roaming her back yard. The chubby old cat acted like she owned the place.

"Good morning Lucy-loo," she sang to the cat, "Did you see what they did to mommy's babies? Did you?" She scratched the cat under its chin and behind its ears while it purred happily. The cat rubbed its body against her robe, leaving mounds of shedding black fur behind.

A police officer eventually showed up, looking bored and resigned to his duties. He took a lengthy statement from my great aunt and we were told that this sort of thing happened a lot. Kids loved smashing garden gnomes – it was what they did. I looked at Mr. Winkles and wished kids these days could be a bit more thorough in their vandalism.

A week later I was back at my great aunt's house and was surprised to see she had several new gnomes scattered across her front yard and in the garden. These didn't look as nice as the old ones, and I wondered where she had gotten them from. They looked cheap and poorly made. The paint on these looked splotchy and the details looked like they had been done by a child. The edges were smudged and uneven. The patterns and colour choices clashed and hurt my eyes if I looked for too long.

I asked her about them and she said they had just appeared there, a new one or two each morning for the past week. This morning there was actually five new ones, she said, with a faraway look in her eyes. She looked tired, like she hadn't been sleeping well. I asked if she was okay and she nodded her head without looking at me, then blinked for a few seconds longer than normal. I asked her if she wanted to go lie down and she said that was a good idea. We decided we would go out shopping the next week, since it wasn't urgent. She had just wanted to get a few gifts for

Christmas – since it was July there wasn't a big hurry, at least in my mind.

The next week I came back and found her passed out on the couch in the living room. She was so tired I could barely wake her up, and almost considered calling an ambulance until she bounced up, looking lively again. She said she had just been napping and was looking forward to our shopping trip. I asked her about the new ranks of gnomes which had begun to make walking to her front door difficult, and she laughed saying that friends had brought them for her. When I asked which friends, she wouldn't say.

Mr. Winkles was waiting for us when we pulled up at the house after shopping. I trudged past him, glaring at him out of the corner of my eye as I carried bags into the house. There was something off about all this, I thought to myself. There was something very wrong going on here. The new gnomes were even more disgusting than the last batch. They were hideous, deformed-looking creatures. They were missing arms and legs, and their faces were twisted and distorted. The features were disproportional and askew.

I felt a sharp pain in my ankle and cried out. I looked down to see my ankle bleeding from a wound. A flap of skin was hanging down unnaturally and blood was trickling down into my sock. I looked over at Mr. Winkles and saw a fresh rivulet of crimson blood running down his axe blade, but when I looked closer there was nothing.

I complained to my great aunt but she said I had likely caught my leg on the railing and just blamed me for not sanding and painting it as I had promised to months ago. I went inside and cleaned the nasty wound, replacing the flap of skin and putting a bandage over it to hold it in place. For a long time it wouldn't stop bleeding – the cut was pretty deep. It took several of the bandages to do the job of covering it and I could still see blood beginning to seep through between the cracks and around the edges.

I went home and continued my research into the eccentric Dutchman who had crafted Mr. Winkles. I had gone down a conspiracy theory rabbit-hole and did not like what I was finding.

A few days later I went back to my great aunt's house. I went by in the late evening, just before she usually went to bed, without calling to tell her that I was coming. I was starting to worry about her, and I had a few bizarre suspicions after my extensive research. I needed to see what was happening there, if only to preserve my own sanity.

When I arrived at her house I parked in the driveway and got out of my car. I heard a low pitched noise from the back yard and went to investigate.

When I got into the back yard, I stopped dead. It was changed completely from the last time I had seen it. The privacy hedges were blocking the public from seeing an oddly terrifying spectacle.

Trees had been cut down and chopped into tiny piles of wood. The back deck had been dismantled, its wood similarly processed and arranged into neat stacks. The most obvious change was that there was now a hoard of hideously deformed lawn gnomes huddled together in the back yard.

I heard the low-pitched sound again and looked to see the cat from next door, Lucy, was being dragged away from the fence, her claws digging into the grass as she tried to save herself. She was being pulled into their midst by about a dozen gnomes, who had tied her with ropes and were pulling her mercilessly towards the center of the fray where a crowd of other gnomes sharpened their glinting knives. The cat howled and made terrified noises, hissing and swatting at the gnomes with her claws.

Mr. Winkles presided over the mayhem, sitting on a misshapen throne carved of driftwood at the back of the lawn. Some gnomes were working at the back of the garden behind him, chopping down another tree and cutting it up into usable pieces. A fire had been constructed and more were huddled around it, roasting what appeared to be mice and squirrels on sticks.

I shouted at them to stop, running into the midst of them, kicking them this way and that, sending their tiny bodies flying. I pulled the ropes off the cat and freed her, as they hacked at my legs with their little knives. I shouted triumphantly when I had finally pulled the last of the ropes off of her, and picked her up in my arms. She kicked with her back legs and dug her sharp claws into my arms, jumping free from me and bounding away quickly. I yelped in pain, clutching my bleeding arms, as the gnomes continued hacking at my legs with their sharp little weapons.

I felt a terrible pain in the back of my head and the world went black.

*

I woke up in a low-ceilinged cave with dirt walls pressed close to my face and cold earth beneath me. I couldn't stand up or even kneel where I was. Claustrophobia gripped me and I felt my chest tighten with fear as I looked around and saw I had less than two feet of room between the floor and the ceiling. I started to hyperventilate as I tried to turn around but found I couldn't. I couldn't even get my hands in front of me.

I realized I was bound and tied up like a sow, with my wrists tied to my ankles. I was being dragged backwards, away from the light. I struggled against the knots and felt them giving way slightly. My only hope was that the things were so defectively inbred it had begun to affect their intelligence and cunning. I pulled with all my strength and felt the ropes give way. I looked behind me and saw the gnomes had fallen backwards, surprised that their tiny string bindings had snapped.

Their wooden faces crunched as I kicked them hard and smashed them with my shoes against the dirt walls of the cave. I crawled forward, dirt flying into my eyes and in my mouth. The gnomes scrambled after me, and attacked my legs with sharp knives. I screamed and flailed at them, batting them away as I made my way on my belly towards the light. Progress was slow but fear of what was behind me drove me forward, and I managed to ignore the pain of their attacks.

I finally clawed grass and pulled myself out onto the back lawn. The cool night air was fresh against my face. I scrambled to my feet and ran over to Mr. Winkles, where he sat in his driftwood throne. He stood up on the chair and pulled out his axe, swinging it menacingly.

I grabbed a flaming log from the fire. It burned my hands and I screamed but held it nonetheless. I flung it with all the force I could muster, hitting Mr. Winkles square in the chest. The flames spread impossibly fast and he lit up like flash-paper. He began to scream and wail, his varnished flesh melting. The other gnomes ran over and threw sand and dirt on him, extinguishing the flames.

I turned around to see my great aunt standing silently behind me. She slid the blade of a very large knife into my belly. The pain was like nothing I had ever felt before. She twisted the knife and it flared up ten times worse. I thought I was going to die, there was no way anyone could live through that pain.

"I told you, no one hurts my babies," she whispered in my ear as I collapsed to the ground, the knife still lodged in my gut.

*

Von Welken had gone insane, the stories said. But there were other stories online too, if you looked deeper. If you probed the dark web for conspiracy theories you could find more than a few people who said there was more going on in that case.

The suicide note, for instance: It had started off in Von Welken's handwriting, but then had veered into childish block letters. In his writing he said he hadn't made the new gnomes. He said that the winking one had made them, and his children had borne more hideous and deformed children. The block letters disagreed, saying Von Welken had made the gnomes, right before he lost his mind. The police had determined the scene unusual but it was ruled a suicide nonetheless.

I wish they had done a bit more digging.

Maybe they wouldn't have put up his gnomes for auction if they had realized what they really were. Then maybe I wouldn't be here, in this tiny dirt cave.

I'm trapped here with nothing but the light from my dying phone to keep me company. I've tried calling the police. They say to stop calling, that the prank isn't funny. They say they've been to my aunt's house and seen her. She says there's nothing wrong, and that she doesn't even have a great-nephew. The police operator says there's no sign of a tunnel at the back of the house. Gnomes are such excellent craftsmen.

No Sleep Tonight / Jordan Grupe

I spent a week on the ocean floor...
I'll never step foot in the sea again

Spending a week at the bottom of the ocean is pretty much as crazy as it sounds. You get into a tin can with a couple other people and they lower you into the ocean. You sink to the sea floor and live in the airspace at the top of the can for a week.

There's not a lot of space when you're breathing fresh air down there, so the only reason to go is if you love to scuba. That's all there is to do down there.

Normally you get an hour of dive-time for each tank of oxygen you're carrying. So every hour you have to go back up to the surface from the bottom of the ocean, which takes time. When you're living down there, it's different. Your dive-time is limited only by your endurance.

We set up fast-refill stations and use high-powered hoses to refill our tanks with oxygen. That way you can stay in the water as long as you want. Hours fly by while you're down there, and you can never get bored. It's a whole different planet on the sea floor, and who wouldn't want to spend all day staring at aliens? Fish of countless varieties swim past, in all the colours of the rainbow. Sea turtles and octopus, dolphins and manta rays, sharks and whales, you'll see it all. Not to mention the unparalleled beauty of the coral reefs and the plethora of lifeforms that dwell symbiotically within them.

The only thing I didn't like was night-time at the bottom of the ocean. You'd look out from the habitat into utter blackness – darker than anything you've ever seen. And how can you not imagine what's out there? We had seen sharks, giant octopus, and barracudas swimming nearby.

There's also everything else your imagination can come up with – everything you've seen on movies and TV that isn't even real. Amphibious humanoids who look like swamp thing, who creep up silently from the kelp and grab your arm with their hands, dotted with suckers like the tentacles of an octopus. Giant krakens and massive dinosaur sharks left over from the Jurassic period and all other manner of nightmares could be out in that darkness. If you spent a week down there, you'd begin to realize too, just how ignorant we are of the world that exists in tandem with ours.

You try to avoid those thoughts when you're out of the habitat at night. You have to leave the habitat to go to the bathroom so there's no avoiding it if you need to go number two.

One night I was awoken by a rumbling in my stomach around 3 AM. It was dark inside the tin can we called home, silent except for the sound of water splashing up against the inside of the hab. My stomach lurched again, this time more urgently. I realized I would need to go outside. I put my mask on but didn't take my regulator or oxygen, since the little hut we used as a toilet wasn't far away, maybe twenty feet. I could easily hold my breath for that long.

The light from the hut gleamed ahead of me as I dove down into the darkness, my mind still foggy with sleep. The dim bulb on the outhouse was the only other light in this universe, so I went to it with urgency, for more than one reason. When I got there, I popped up into the little air bubble inside and pulled down my trunks. I had made it just in time.

Pretty soon fish were coming by for their morning meal and I swatted at them with my hand, trying to pinch it off before they could burrow their little faces further into my ass crack. Fucking fish just love to eat shit.

As if that wasn't nightmare enough, there was that blackness. All around except for the light from the outhouse and the one from the habitat. The darkness stretched out forever and was infinite in its mystery. I wondered how far away the nearest great white shark was and if they would be attracted to the scent of all the smaller fish. I shook my head and tried to think of anything else. It was completely silent except for my breathing and the sound of water splashing gently against the inside of the hut.

I finally pulled up my trunks, slapping a fish with my hand as I did so, and waited for a minute for the air to clear, so to speak. No sense rushing the dive back into the blackness, I thought, especially considering what I'd just polluted it with.

After a minute, I took a breath and popped back into the water from the air bubble. I swam towards the light of the habitat. When I was not even halfway there, both lights flickered and went out. I was immediately disoriented. My foggy mind had just been asleep a few minutes ago and I wished I had taken longer to wake up before venturing out alone. I hadn't even woken anyone else up to tell them I was going.

The after-image of the glow from the habitat still danced in my vision, so I followed it, my heart beating fast and heavy in my chest. I felt terrified and hoped I was heading in the right direction. I followed my instincts and training and tried to ignore the part of my brain that told me I might not be going the right way. I felt something large brush against my hand and recoiled in shock.

What the hell was that, I wondered. I was suddenly picturing a giant hammerhead right in front of me, instead of the habitat. My panic intensified. My vision was starting to go a bit red around the edges and I wondered how much time I had wasted. It was a good thing I could hold my breath for a long time.

I tried to swim in the direction of the habitat but I suddenly wasn't sure which way it was anymore. The thing that had brushed against my hand had felt large and it had scared me more than a bit. Kicking with my flippers, I began swimming in the direction I thought was right.

My hand brushed up against it again, whatever it was. This time it was on the other side of me. I tried to ignore my fear and kept kicking my legs, my vision was beginning to flood with redness and I was really starting to feel true dread and fear bloom inside me like

I had never felt before. Every part of me was screaming for air. I tried to calm my mind and remember my training.

My hand grabbed onto something and in my confused and oxygen-deprived state I mistook it for a power line, running to the outhouse. I began to pull myself along the misshapen tube. It seemed to squirm and writhe in my grip, but I continued along nonetheless, hoping it would lead me back to the habitat. As I got closer, I felt more of the weird organically shaped tubes. They felt lumpy and had spikes and divots here and there. I realized with disgust that they were definitely not oxygen or electrical lines. They seemed to stick to my hands when I grabbed onto them, not wanting to let go. I had to pry my hand off the last time and decided to stop touching them altogether.

Just as I was about to lose all hope, my left hand brushed up against the hard metallic edge of the habitat. I had almost gone by it, I realized with a wave of horrified relief. I had almost swam right past it and out into the open water.

I felt the shape of it and managed to correct my path. I popped my head up into the habitat and gasped for air, panting and coughing up water from my lungs. I climbed out of the water and managed to find the ladder leading up to my bunk.

"FUCK! I almost died out there just now!" I yelled, and was surprised when no one woke up to ask if I was okay.

I felt new fear well up inside me, thinking of all the tangled organisms that had been all over the outside of the habitat. What the hell were those things, and why wasn't anyone talking or waking up inside the hab?

I rummaged through my things, and pulled out my flashlight, wishing I had brought it with me earlier. How stupid. If I had died I would have deserved it.

I turned the light on and screamed. There was no rational explanation for what I saw inside the habitat.

The other two members of my crew were surrounded by what appeared to be misshapen tentacles. But, no that's not quite right. Not tentacles, these were different. The long tubular shapes that came up out of the water reminded me of a recent article about a siphonophore that had been discovered off the coast of Australia. It was now recorded as the longest creature ever seen by man. It was really a collection of zooids that came together and cloned itself thousands upon thousands of times to create an infinitely long "silly-string" that could stretch for hundreds of meters. The crew had called it akin to an underwater galaxy, and pictures of the siphonophore looked otherworldly. It went on forever – a twisting, spiralling organism that faded off into the distant ocean with no end in sight.

This was like that, only much worse. This siphonophore appeared to have mutated, and it had picked up some new abilities never seen before in all my research.

The thing had absorbed other marine life somehow. I saw barracuda with sharp teeth, small sharks, and eels, their eyes wide and terrified, opening and closing their mouths. They were covered with a thin membrane and appeared to have been attached to the thing against their will. They were now prisoners of it, being dragged along by the massive, ropey sea creature.

My crew had the tentacle things all around them, choking them at their necks and wrapped around their bodies and arms. The white flesh of the thing was spreading across them quickly, wrapping them up in its slimy sheath. My crewmate, Mike, tried to scream but his voice was muffled as I saw a vine of siphonophore crawl down his throat, planting little roots as it went.

I was terrified, hyperventilating. I ducked back into the furthest corner of my bunk and watched in horror as the thing consumed my crew mates rapidly, and attached itself to them. I watched as it pulled them under and dragged them down into the ocean, their eyes still wide and afraid. Would it filter the ocean water through its gills so they could live down there, I wondered. Would it provide oxygen to the new members of the colony, or would it just consume them for fuel and move on?

No one would have believed me if I told them what happened. So I said it was a diving accident. I told them I tried to save Mike and Beth, and there wasn't anything I could do. A search party had turned up nothing, as I had expected.

When I got back to the surface I told my family I would never step foot in the sea again. They think it's because I'm remorseful. They think I just feel bad about Mike and Beth, but that's not it. I feel bad about them, sure, but what I really think about is what's down there, under the surface. I saw how fast that thing consumed them. I think about the transatlantic garbage patch and how that was the big problem for a while. I think we might have a new problem now.

I now know why no one sleeps in room 14

I couldn't understand why the charge nurse gave me such a strange look when I said I was going into room 14 to take a nap on my break.

It wasn't unusual for us to occasionally roll a stretcher into one of the rooms to sleep for an hour or so during break on a night shift. We work 12 hours straight and just take one long break in the middle so we can actually get a decent nap in.

"I guess... If you want to," she said, her brow furrowed.

"Oh, Sharon! He's new. He doesn't know about it," Jodie, another nurse said cryptically.

Sharon, the charge nurse turned and looked at her, "Ha! You're right! I guess nobody's told you yet," she said, turning back to me.

"What? What's the deal with room 14?" I asked. Now I was curious. It was the only room on the floor we had available.

The other staff on break were already sound asleep in their assigned sleeping cubbies (conference rooms, storage rooms, you name it, we'd roll a stretcher in there and nap our brains out).

47

"Well, everybody who works here knows it's haunted," Sharon said.

I thought she was kidding, obviously. Serious people don't believe in ghosts. People like Sharon, who was as sensible as they come, definitely didn't believe in ghosts.

"Really," I chuckled. I didn't believe in ghosts at all. I knew everything that people claimed had some rational explanation. I had seen a documentary about it once. It was fascinating how people came up with things in their minds and would remember them later and elaborate on them, making them more fantastic, adding characters like ghosts to make them seem more exciting. All a bunch of pathological liars, like the people who claim to be abducted by UFOs, or so I thought.

"You guys seriously believe in that stuff?" I asked with a laugh.

They both looked at each other, sending psychic messages back and forth. I had only been working there for a bit so I hadn't developed that particular talent yet.

Also, I didn't know the one thing all new nurses should know – listen to the people who have been doing it longer than you. They almost always know better than you do. Especially when you're really new, which I was.

"I mean, if you don't believe us, you can give it a shot…"

"Guys! No! Seriously, that's not okay." A voice in the corner chimed in, Liang, a guy who had also worked there for a while. "You really should not sleep in there, Jason. It's not good a place to sleep."

I usually trusted Liang, so I was a bit disappointed he was joining in on this apparent prank on the newbie to the floor. Maybe one of them just wanted to sleep in there themselves, so they were trying to psych me out, I thought.

"Okay, guys, I get it, I'm the new guy. But seriously, I think I'll be okay. I'm really not worried."

Liang tried again to convince me, growing more desperate, but I blew him off, thinking he was just taking the joke too far. Sharon and Jodie had given up and were sitting there silently, waiting to see what would happen.

I laughed self-consciously and went to the clean supply room to grab some blankets and brought them into the room. It was a semi-private room with two beds. They were both clean, so I figured I would just change the sheets when I was done and forget about rearranging the room to pull in a stretcher, this would be easier, and I was dead tired.

I turned off the lights and lay down in the bed closest to the door. The room was silent and dark. I let my mind drift off to sleep.

I had a terrible dream. I dreamt that someone was standing over me, watching me sleep. I knew exactly where I was and felt awake but really I was still asleep. I tried to lift my arms but found they wouldn't move.

I felt paralyzed and filled with dread as I tried to look up and to my right where the thing stood but couldn't. I could only see a dark vague outline of something large and malevolent. I heard the thing speaking angrily, and it began to shout, but I couldn't understand its words. My heart began to race as I realized this thing wanted me out!

I tried to stand up but found I couldn't. I began to panic as time went on and the thing became more and more angry. It was a horrifying feeling to be unable to move, to be suddenly incapable of it. I started to become more terrified as the thing began moving in, screaming in my face, closer and closer. I started to thrash about in the bed, finally, mercifully waking up.

I realized I had been asleep and had dreamt the whole thing. The whole thing had been a product of my overworked, overstressed mind.

But why, then, did I still feel such panic and utter dread? It felt as if I could die at any moment.

The room was silent and dark for a few more moments. Then I heard someone clear their throat next to me in the pitch black room. I felt a chill run down my spine and goosebumps spread across my entire body. The curtain beside me had been pulled across while I was asleep, separating me from the bed next to me.

I wanted to believe it was another nurse that had come in and closed the curtain so they could sleep in the other bed, but I knew that wasn't it. I could already tell something was wrong.

I had to see. I pulled out my cell and turned on the flashlight. I looked beside me, terrified. Nothing at first, and then.. I saw a hand, gnarled and bleeding, green and black and rotten, pull back the curtain from beside me. The face which stared back at me was not human. It was something evil, something which had gotten in here which was not supposed to be here at all. It was an abomination, a terrible, wrong thing in a place that should be meant for peace and healing.

I screamed so loudly I woke up the entire floor of sleeping patients.

I ran from the room, falling over and bruising my hip badly in the process, getting tangled up in the laundry bin near the doorway.

I fled and left the hospital entirely. I've never gone back. I can't bear to be in the same building with that thing. Now that I know it's there, I can never be in that hospital again. I could certainly never be a patient there.

When I thought about it later, I realized the patients had always told us they had trouble sleeping in that room. I would call up the doctor and ask for some melatonin or some Zopiclone, maybe a lorazepam if it came down to it. But now I understand the real reason why no one could ever sleep in room 14.

No Sleep Tonight / Jordan Grupe

I visited an abandoned penitentiary

I was a small child of about eight years old when we went to visit Pillsenburg Prison, so you would think my recollections of that day would be hazy. But they are burnt into my memory permanently – like a scar on my mind that will never heal.

The old penitentiary was a well-known tourist trap, I would find out later in life. I did a lot of research after what happened. I'm sure you would too. It turned out a few other people had paranormal experiences there, although no one else ever went missing.

I also found a few web pages dedicated to the old prison, describing it as haunted. The giant fortress-like building was made of grey stone, mined from a nearby quarry over 150 years ago.

My family had distant relatives visiting from Europe, and we had run out of standard touristy crap to do, so we had gone a bit off the beaten path and chosen to take a tour of the oldest penitentiary in the country, which was only a couple hours away. My dad's cousin stayed at home, saying he was tired and to go without him, but his son Gunter decided he would come along.

Gunter was a year older than I was at the time, and a precocious little brat. He would ask pointed questions in his perfect English, not a trace of German accent to be found, and then would have the nerve to second-guess you and correct you when you gave him the answer.

He was a mouthy little know-it-all, and I was looking forward to having him out of my bedroom. He had taken over my bed and I had been forced to sleep on the hard wooden floor, a victim of my parents' politeness.

The tour started outside in the courtyard where the prisoners had exercised. The guide pointed out features here and there as a dozen of us unlucky souls trailed lackadaisically behind him.

The giant building loomed over us, dark and foreboding, blocking out the sun and leaving us chilly in the morning air.

I didn't want to go inside, I had already realized, but my parents were walking towards the entrance, leaving me behind.

Gunter was up front with the tour-guide, prodding him with repeated questions and correcting him when he made a minor error, pointing at the brochure in his hands.

I hurried and followed them inside, trying to ignore the feelings of dread as the dark entryway swallowed me up like the gaping maw of a grey stone giant.

When we got inside we went through several sets of steel bar cages. The guide explained these were screening points for new prisoners. His descriptions were vivid and I felt like I could hear and see the images he described of terrified prisoners being heckled by the guards and other inmates as they were marched in, shivering naked as the day they were born, hosed down and cavity-searched. My mom covered my ears at this little detail and I swatted her hands away.

As we continued along, I heard the tour guide make a snappy remark at Gunter, "Why don't you lead the tour you little smart-ass?" or something along those lines. Gunter walked back to us, looking momentarily dejected. Then he quickly remembered he could annoy me as well and perked up again.

"Did you know the prisoners here had to work on chain gangs? Do you know what chain gangs are, Jayson?" He pointed at the brochure and poked me in the ribs. I said of course I knew what chain gangs were. Regardless, he spent the next ten minutes explaining what they were to me, speaking loudly over the frustrated objections of the tour guide.

We continued on into an old cell-block. The guide explained how the prisoners would line up for inspection, and their shoes were expected to be polished to a mirror-shine. He explained how new prisoners would be hazed, their shoes scuffed while they slept by their bunkmate, so that they would fail the morning inspection. No excuses would be tolerated, and they would be confined to the cell for the remainder of the day. It was no wonder cell-mate murders and suicides had reached record levels there.

We went down some stairs and into the lower levels, where we were told the cafeteria was located. I had an image of food and my stomach rumbled. I licked my lips and realized my throat was dry as well. A drink would be nice, I thought. But the guide went on to explain how no food or beverages were served on the premises any longer, that this was simply an old cafeteria used by prisoners. I grumbled something to my dad about how hungry I was, and he said we would get something to eat in an hour or two, after we left the prison.

Gunter stopped me for a moment. He grabbed my wrist and pulled me back, away from the group. He said he had brought a few snacks along. I was suddenly warming up to my distant relative, I thought. He pulled out some German gummy bears and poured a few into my hands. We chewed them and looked around at our surroundings. The tour guide's voice got quieter and quieter as we were left behind. I wasn't worried at the time, thinking we would just run and catch up to them in a minute.

Gunter started prattling on about something again and I started getting anxious. He wouldn't shut up and ignored my body language saying I wanted to move along. Finally he finished what he was saying and I dragged him down the hallway. He seemed to take pleasure in my annoyance and I began to dislike him again immediately.

He dragged his feet as I pulled him along, stopping and pointing out mundane things to purposefully bother me further. I furrowed my brow, thinking it was odd I could no longer hear the group up ahead.

We turned the corner and I was surprised to note the scents of coffee and porridge wafting through the air. Odd, I thought, since the tour guide had said they no longer served food there.

I heard voices from a doorway to the right, up ahead. It sounded like a crowd of hundreds of people, their voices a low-pitched buzz.

We walked up to the doorway and I stopped immediately. Gunter bumped into me and spilled a few of his gummy bears. He punched me in the arm but I didn't even feel it. He turned and looked as well and dropped the whole bag of candy on the floor, spilling the colourful little laxative bear bodies everywhere.

Both of us stood in the doorway, in complete shock. The room ahead of us was full of hundreds of prisoners. Their black and white striped uniforms were all identical. Their heads were shaved and their bodies packed shoulder to shoulder at the long tables were they sat eating gummy-looking porridge and black coffee.

To one side of the room a long line of prisoners were lined up, shuffling trays along a serving line and getting spoonfuls of slop ladled into their bowls by unsympathetic men dressed in white.

Gunter began to walk through the doorway, as if in a daze. I got a bad feeling, watching him. It was as if I could sense that his walking through that threshold was a crossing-over. And I knew then that he should not cross over.

I chased after him, grabbing his wrist. He was bigger than me, though. He looked back at me with a mischievous grin and pulled me through, laughing.

It felt immediately different on the other side of the doorway. The voices of the prisoners rose to a deafening roar and the smells became definite and real. I could now detect the burnt undertones of the coffee, and the sweat and body odour of the many prisoners who stood all around us.

I looked up and saw a big man with broad shoulders and a crooked smile. His bald head gleamed and I saw he was missing several teeth. He looked like a very bad man.

He grabbed me by my biceps and his fingers dug in painfully. I tried to call out but he covered my mouth, looking around quickly. He pulled me out of the big room with little effort, my feet dragging over the stone floor.

I looked over and saw Gunter had been grabbed by a couple of other prisoners who held him tight and covered his mouth. His eyes were wide and afraid.

They dragged us through another doorway and into a cell block. No one was around and it seemed like everyone was preoccupied with breakfast in the big cafeteria.

There were four of them and they pulled us into a cell, with hungry looks in their eyes. The man with the missing teeth pulled out a crudely-made shank and held it up to Gunter's neck. He was struggling the hardest since he was bigger, and they decided to deal with him first.

"What the hell are we doing, Charlie," the one prisoner said to the man with the missing teeth. "These are kids. How did they even get in here?"

Charlie backhanded the other man and sent him reeling. He staggered back and turned his face against the wall, rubbing his reddened cheek.

"If Johnny in't keen enough to see the upside 'ere, I dunno what ta tell ye gents," the man with the missing teeth said, digging the blade in deeper. "But I kin tell ye exactly what we's gonna din. We's gonna use these lads as bargaining chips. They's gonna be our ticket outta 'ere."

The other two men looked at him dubiously. They bickered back and forth a bit but reluctantly agreed to give it a shot. They were all sentenced to life, so they saw no downside, from what I could overhear. The man with the missing teeth became a bit distracted by the conversation, and his blade drifted further and further from Gunter's neck. His hand crept closer to his mouth, inadvertently.

Suddenly, Gunter twisted his head and bit down hard on Charlie's hand. He screamed in pain and dropped the knife. Gunter thrashed and wriggled his head, his mouth filling with blood as his teeth dug deeper and deeper into the man's hand.

The other three men grabbed my distant cousin and held him down as he kicked and wailed. They covered his mouth and made a hasty gag out of a pillow case. I saw Charlie nursing his wounds and made the mistake of looking him in the eyes. He caught me looking and his stare burnt into me like the sun. He was going to teach us a lesson, he said.

Gunter was crying as he was held down and restrained painfully. They forced him to watch as Charlie picked up the dirty shank from the floor and walked over to me. He told me this is how it works here. If one man's shoes are scuffed, the bunk mate has to spend the whole day in the cell with him too, it's a mutual punishment. But worth it to show a new prisoner his place. They were going to show us our place, he said.

He took the dirty shank and I watched, horrified, as they held out my hand and extended my fingers. The missing-tooth man began to saw away with the blunt and filthy blade, making slow progress as he hacked off my pinky finger. It was slow work with the crude instrument. He finally reached bone and it took another few minutes to get through that. I passed out from the pain at least once, probably more.

When that finger was fully removed, he moved over to the other side and did the same thing there. The blade became blunter as he worked and I screamed and screamed through the hands, which muffled my voice. The man behind me twisted my neck painfully with every sound I made and choked me with his forearm across my neck.

With both my smallest fingers removed, the man walked over to Gunter. He waved the fingers in his face and the blood flew and splattered on him.

"Aye, lookit what ye did! This be yer fault, ye little swine. Fek yerself," the man said, and threw the severed fingers at Gunter's face. He took the blunt blade and plunged it into Gunter's belly. Blood spurted into the air and all over the stone floor as he removed the blade and reinserted it several more times, slowly and methodically. His friends began to look around anxiously and I wondered how much more time was left before prisoners and guards began to return from the meal.

Gunter collapsed to the floor with a loud thud, his head crashing against the steel bars of the cage door. The men kneeled over him for a second, checking to make sure he was still alive, and I sensed my chance. It would probably be my only opportunity to escape, so I went for it.

I curled my bloody hands into eight-fingered fists and punched Charlie square in the biscuits. He went down to his knees and clutched himself, cursing me and screaming. By the time the other men had turned around, though, I was already running past them.

My small size worked to my advantage and I managed to duck past their reaching hands as they tried to grab me. I sprinted from the cell, back down towards the cafeteria, blood pouring from the places where my fingers used to be.

I got back to the cafeteria and saw prisoners were beginning to file out. Several of them saw me and gave surprised looks, pointing and exclaiming. The old slang they used sounded a hundred years old, and I didn't understand half of what they were saying.

I ran past the crowd and managed to get back to the open door, the portal we had come through that had somehow transported us back a century or more. It shimmered and looked glassy and surreal. I started to step through, and stopped, not of my own volition.

The hand that grabbed me belonged to a guard, I saw. His blue uniform was neatly pressed, the brass buttons on his vest gleaming. His grip was iron on my arm.

"Haud th' trolley, laddie. Urr ye stealin' fae the scullery? Is that it? Ah cannae let ye lea sea quick." He began to pull me away from the door and my feet dragged on the stone floor as I wailed and hollered.

"Ah will ne'er ken howfur ye managed tae git in 'ere, bairn. Deh ye hae parents, wee yin? Urr ye an orphan or juist an eejit?" He looked down at my hands and finally noticed my fingers.

"Bugger that's ferr an injury! Whit happened tae yer' fingers wee yin?"

I tried to tell him I just needed to go through the doorway, just to take me to the doorway. But he wouldn't listen. Panicking, I kicked him in his shin. His grip stayed firm and his eyes turned cold.

"Ye wee bas ah will murdurr ye fur that," he said, and pulled out the club from the holster at his waist.

He swung it at me and hit me in the knee. I felt it shatter and collapsed to the ground instantly.

I looked up at him and saw he was saying something about how I deserved it. That was when Charlie came up behind him. He took the dull knife and made a quick red line appear across the guard's throat. The man dropped his club and clutched his neck, blood pouring out from the gaps between his fingers.

I tried to crawl away, but looked back and saw the gap-toothed man standing over me. His broad face was red and full of fury. He plunged the shank down, into my leg. Pain flared up all anew and my adrenaline kicked into overdrive. My pituitary gland tried desperately to drown out the pain with endorphins, but was only partially successful.

Several prisoners grabbed Charlie from behind suddenly, cursing at him, saying that no one should hurt a kid. I couldn't believe it They were going to save me.

I crawled away from them, dragging my shattered knee behind me and my other leg with the stab wound as well. My unfortunate finger-stumps left pools of blood on the grey stone as I pulled myself towards the shimmering doorway ahead.

I finally reached it and pulled myself through to the other side.

It was a while before anyone found me. And they never found Gunter. I tried to tell them what had happened but no one believed me. The story is pretty far-fetched, I know. Time traveling is generally considered by most people to be impossible. I guess I'm no longer most people.

Everyone told me I was lying and needed to start being truthful. To this day, most of my family will no longer talk to me, except for my parents. But this is the truth.

I mean, why would I shatter my own kneecap, cut off both my pinky fingers, and plunge a blunt homemade knife into my own leg? Unless I was completely bonkers I would never do that. Am I completely bonkers?

We were told not to break quarantine

We weren't supposed to leave town, the government orders were very specific about that. No travel between regions was allowed since the virus death rates had begun to climb again.

The world had been struggling to recover as the virus had slowly receded. Life as we knew it had begun to resume as normal, with the addition of masks and social distancing. A vaccine had been fast-tracked and would be out in a year to a year and half.

We all relaxed and let down our guard pretty quickly, thinking the masks and watered-down hand sanitizer would keep us safe. The economy reopened quicker than expected, against the warnings of infectious disease experts. Those experts quickly proved to be right, as the rates of infection suddenly skyrocketed again.

As a security guard in a medium/high security mental health hospital, I was deemed essential, so I had been continuing my full-time shifts. I patrolled the hospital grounds, responded to code whites (violent patients), searched for missing patients (code yellows) and documented everything in my trusty notepad. It helped at the end of the day when I wrote my Shift Summary Report to have exact times and details written down to help fill in any blanks in my memory.

I had been working full time for about two years so I had managed to accrue a bit of vacation time and by mid-summer decided to take a trip up to the family cottage.

I had booked the time off long before, but had been debating whether we should go. The hospital wasn't any busier than usual, in fact they had been discharging people much more quickly than normal. They were pushing people out to try to reduce the effects of a potential outbreak within the hospital. All non-violent patients who could be treated safely on an outpatient basis were given the boot. The halls of many units that had been full of patients just months before were now empty, and very spooky to patrol, especially at night.

There were several problems with going to the cottage. First of all, it was illegal. The government still had orders in place stating no one could leave their designated region without express permission. There were hot spots where the virus was out of control. Our family cottage was five hours away, and well outside our region. We would have to pass through several different jurisdictions to reach it. We lived in a hot spot, the cottage community was a cold spot. The TV showed maps in red and blue with shades of orange and yellow in between. Red for hot, blue for cold.

In the news they were reporting about small cottage communities becoming tribal and militaristic about their territory in some places, especially remote blue regions where the virus hadn't yet spread and where hospitals and life-saving supplies like ventilators were scarce. I had gone up to my cottage every year for my entire life, I knew the people up near our cottage to be friendly and neighbourly, so I wasn't worried. *Just the news trying to show the worst of everything,* I thought.

We resolved that we would stop only when necessary and take all the supplies we needed along with us. There would be no reason to go to the small town up near our cottage where we usually went for groceries, coffee, or bait when we were up there. I didn't see any harm in it, and we really needed to get out of the city for a while; our apartment was suffocating. There was no green space nearby, and we didn't even have a balcony. The windows were tiny and we were on the top floor of an ancient and poorly ventilated building. All the heat from the floors below rose up to us as we steamed like dim sum in the wooden basket that was our 11th floor apartment.

We had gotten up to the cottage without incident, relieved not to have been pulled over by any police, since we had no real cover story for our trip and would have been fined and sent back home. I had used an app on my phone which showed police locations to avoid roadblocks.

Our cottage is off the beaten path to say the least. I had one friend admit to me half-jokingly that he thought just maybe I was taking him out into the woods to murder him after I brought him up for his first trip. It was late at night by the time we had gotten up there. Without the benefit of the text I sent him I'll try to recreate its contents, which were probably slightly less creepy than this.

Directions after the highway are as follows:

Turn right onto the gravel road from the paved highway. Veer left, continuing past a cemetery where the road turns to washboard-textured dirt, turn left after five miles then proceed carefully through the twisting hair pin turns through the dark moonless forest, turn left onto a laneway of two barely visible dirt tracks through long grass, twisting and turning with not a soul in sight in the pitch-black night, up steep hills and back down the other side, left again at the gate of what appears to be a walking path, do not fret about the water only inches from the tires of the car as you pass through low points where crickets chirp and bullfrogs bellow, finally, with increasing bumpiness drive forward until you think, "this isn't possibly a road anymore," and you'll arrive at a small shack at the end of a drive, with still black water on all sides, a peninsula just narrow enough for a driveway and a cottage with a small deck and fire pit area at the back, where I have spent many happy summers.

No running water and only a small marine battery with limited juice for electricity. Kerosene oil lamps flickering in the corners and spiders nesting all around with the odd mouse or two scampering in the shadows. I loved it.

The only thing that I didn't like about the place was the toilet situation. The outhouse was a problem that my procrastinating family had been planning and negotiating how to remedy for years. The ramshackle hut which served as our toilet had been standing askew at the end of the driveway for decades, after my grandfather had built it many years before. Snakes and squirrels nested in it and giant spiders made webs inside in the most inconvenient places. I always felt like something was going to bite me from the ancient human waste pit below my exposed ass as I sat on the poorly secured and splintering toilet seat. The worst part was there was no light or window so when you closed the door it was pitch black in there. All you had to see by was the starlight through the gaps in wood slats on the outhouse walls unless you had a dim, ancient flashlight pilfered from the cottage store-room.

We got up there late at night and the mosquitos were ferocious. I pulled up my hood and dashed in and out of the cottage, bringing in luggage until it was all inside. My wife was already wiping down tables with disinfectant and tidying up. Mouse poop was scattered here and there and everywhere. I took out the broom and began to sweep.

Eventually the place was tidy enough that we could sit down and relax after our long drive. I opened the cooler and grabbed a beer and Christine surprised me by doing the same. She doesn't usually drink at all and I drink rarely, although slightly more at the cottage.

The place always had a spooky feeling when you first arrived there at night. We were so isolated there, and it was so *quiet,* especially contrasted with the constant noise of the car on the road and the never-ending noise of the city. I checked my phone for the time (11:15 PM) and saw I had no cell signal.

That's strange, I thought.

We'd had pretty good service up there since several years before when they had installed a cell tower close enough to reach us on clear days, and tonight was as clear as they came.

We sat on the couch in the tiny old living room and drank our beer. There wasn't much to do up there after dark, especially since we didn't feel like building a fire. Christine pulled out the laptop and we watched an old episode of *Community* while we talked.

"Weird that there's no signal up here all of a sudden, I guess no Netflix tonight," I said.

"I downloaded a bunch of stuff before we left," she said. I breathed a sigh of relief. We had brought our auxiliary laptop and last I had checked it was dangerously low on content.

We had been snacking while we talked for a bit and my always troublesome stomach started to gurgle and do backflips, signaling an urgent need to hit the bathroom. Hesitantly I made my way outside and began the fifty yard walk to the outhouse.

I turned off my flashlight to admire the stars up above and let my eyes adjust to the darkness. The moonless night was beautiful. The sky above came into focus as my eyes adjusted and I saw the Milky Way start to appear in all its glory. Billions, trillions, of individual stars of varying sizes and shapes stood out against a background of milky white, which featured prominently in the sky. Details you could never see decently from the city.

Fireflies lit up intermittently in the distance ahead of me. My stomach gurgled again and I continued on, reminding myself to be careful not to trip walking blindly over the uneven ground toward the outhouse.

I paused outside the outhouse in the silent darkness of the forest. In the distance a coyote howled. I braced myself for what was behind the door and opened the hook latch. I shone the flashlight inside and walked in, turned around, pulled down my pants, and began to sit down. I looked to my left and screamed.

A large family of bats had taken up residence inside the rickety old outhouse and were hanging from the ceiling in the corner, their eyes glinting red in my flashlight beam. There were dozens of them inside the outhouse with me, and I suddenly noticed their sticky, oozing guano covering every surface on that side of the outhouse. They woke up and began to beat their wings and shriek, swooping down at me and all around me, nipping at my face and neck.

I jumped out of the outhouse, my pants halfway off and the flashlight still laying inside on the nasty guano-covered ledge beside the old beat-up toilet seat. I crawled away and pulled up my pants to run, zipping them up as I went. Blood trickled down my face as I hurried inside.

"Oh my God! What happened to you?! Are you okay?" Christine jumped up and ran over to me when I came inside. I told her what had happened and she led me over to the couch to sit down.

She grabbed a fresh bottle of water from nearby and poured it over the tiny bite marks and scratches covering my face and neck.

We decided the only logical course of action was to head to the nearest hospital. I needed a rabies shot and some disinfectant on my wounds, immediately.

We got into the car and Christine drove down the nauseating road through the forest to the nearest town, Bronze Lake, where they had a very small 24-hour medical center. The fact we were in the area illegally crossed our minds, but neither of us chose to bring it up. If the hospital decided to call the police, the worst they'd do is fine us and send us home, we hoped.

When we got to the hospital it was quiet, dark, and empty, save for a few cars and a buzzing red fluorescent cross which lit up the parking lot. We walked up to the doors and saw a sign hanging there which instructed us to sanitize our hands and put on a mask from the dispenser to the right. We did so and a woman appeared unbidden at the glass door.

The woman who answered the door turned out to be the nurse. She looked us up and down from behind her mask and face shield, took our temperatures with a thermometer gun, and grudgingly let us inside after we explained what had happened and begged her for a rabies shot and some alcohol to clean my wounds.

The doctor came in an hour later, clearly annoyed at having been called in from home during the night.

"Who do you think you people are, anyways," he asked, frowning as he stabbed me in the ass with a giant needle, a horrible pain running down my leg from my buttocks, causing my knee to buckle. They had seen my ID and didn't appear to be calling the police, but they were pissed off, I could tell that much.

"You know, you're coming from one of those hot spots, one of the *hottest spots* in the country, and you come up here to our community, bringing God only knows what germs and viruses with you.." He trailed off. I couldn't help but feel guilty but also a bit angry. It's not like we were *dirty* or something. We had a right to visit our own property, didn't we? To check on it and make sure it was okay?

I didn't say anything though, I just nodded my head feebly and apologized, saying we were just checking on a plumbing issue and would be heading back the next day.

He didn't seem to buy any of what I was saying, and so he just finished what he was doing and left, leaving his dirty needles and supplies for the nurse to clean up. She came in looking even angrier than before and told us to get out as she began noisily cleaning up the exam room.

We got back into our car and I turned it on, backed out of our parking spot, and headed back to the cottage...

 After a few minutes of driving I looked in the rear view mirror and saw the headlights behind us.

It was unusual to see anyone on the roads at this hour of night *before* the pandemic, and since then it had been deserted everywhere. We had barely seen another car on the road even in broad daylight. So it startled me a bit when the car began to follow us down our winding way back to the cottage. The gravel road continued on for a while, with houses on both sides of the road where locals lived. Handmade signs were posted here and there on lawns but I couldn't make them out in the darkness. I assumed they were inspirational messages to first responders and health care workers, as had become the familiar trend.

I tried not to worry too much about the car behind us, it was probably just a local, on their way home from somewhere or other.

But as we got closer and the car followed us down each turn, I began to get worried.

"Is that car following us?" my wife asked.

"I'm not sure," I said, trying not to scare her by sounding calmer than I was.

I slowed down to a crawl, begging the car to pass me, but it stayed stubbornly behind me, its headlights now blindingly bright as it pulled closer and closer to my bumper.

I remembered a tip I had heard somewhere. *If you think someone is following you, pull over.*

I told Christine what I planned to do and I pulled over to the side of the narrow road, opening my window slightly and waving the car behind us past.

The car pulled over behind us. It just sat there with its headlights on and for a moment I couldn't tell what was happening behind us, the headlights in my mirrors were so bright.

The car suddenly pulled away from the side of the road and sped away. I tried to get a look inside but couldn't see through the tinted windows of the old yellow Dodge Neon that drove past.

We waited for a few minutes, trying to tell ourselves it had been nothing, just another car on the road. But we were both freaked out to say the least.

After waiting for a while I started driving again. The dust from the car, which had been following us, still hung in the air and we drove through it as we proceeded onward. We chatted nervously as I drove, trying to talk about something, *anything* else, other than what had just happened.

"I think that doctor hit a nerve with that damn needle," I said.

"Oh no," Christine said soothingly, "Are you alright?"

"Yeah, I think I'll be okay, it just feels a bit numb all the way down my leg. Not a good feeling at all."

"Do you want me to drive," Christine asked.

"Nah, I'm alright, it's not that bad," I said. In truth it didn't feel good at all, but I didn't want to stop again and I definitely didn't want to get out of the safety of the car right now, even for a second.

"Okay, If you're sure," she said, looking worried.

We finally made it back to the driveway of our place, just two dirt tracks in the grass, barely wide enough for a car. I hadn't noticed when it happened but the cloud of dust which was hanging in the air from the yellow Dodge had disappeared suddenly and the air was clear again. The car had pulled into a property along the way somewhere, there were no crossroads in this area of the woods.

I turned into the driveway and drove up the long and winding road towards the cottage.

We got inside and locked the doors behind us. I told Christine I was exhausted and ready for bed and she agreed. We pulled out the futon and made the bed quickly before lying down and tossing and turning restlessly.

Neither of us could sleep despite the late hour, we were both on edge. The cottage was completely silent until we heard a noise coming from outside.

KKKKRRRRR SHH - KKKKRRRRR SHH - KKKKRRRRR SHH

"What *is* that?" Christine sat up in the darkness.

Whatever it was it sounded familiar. It was a noise I had heard a thousand times before, but what was it? It sounded like it was coming from the front of the cottage.

KKKRRRRRR SHH - KKKRRRRRR SHH

The noise continued on like that for a while and we were both too afraid to go outside and look. You ever hear a sound late at night when there's no one around and you're home alone and think, *that noise sounded like it came from a **person**,* but it couldn't have been, there was no one home and that noise had come from the basement, those footsteps, that cough, that silent tapping of an impatient foot, it was all in your head, it had to be. That was what this noise was like.

Finally I placed the sound, but that didn't make me feel any better. At first I didn't want to tell Christine but I had to get a second opinion, she would tell me I was crazy, I hoped.

"Does that noise- Sorry, are you still awake?"

"Of course I'm awake, that noise is freaking me out so much right now."

"Okay, just tell me I'm crazy. Does that noise sound like… digging? Like someone *digging* with a shovel?"

She grabbed me and sat bolt upright, bringing me with her.

"That's it! Oh my God what, why, why would anyone be digging outside our cabin right now!?"

We huddled together. I had no answer for her. We had no weapons aside from a little pocket knife I brought with me to cut fishing line. I hoped I was wrong about the noise. I tried to think what else it could be but came up empty.

The noise continued on methodically for a long time. Whatever hole the person out there was digging, it was large, assuming I wasn't wrong about the sound. I checked my phone periodically for signal, hoping maybe for a bar or two to call 9-1-1. "NO SERVICE" stayed stubbornly embedded at the top of my screen.

After an hour or so the noise finally stopped.

We both lay awake, our eyes fixed on the ceiling, unsure of what to do, waiting for the light of morning when the world outside would be a less terrifying place, we hoped. Sleep was out of the question. I told Christine I wanted to leave as soon as possible, I was sure of that much.

Finally, we began to see dim light outside and we could hear birds singing mutedly through the glass of the windows.

We didn't hear anything for a while, and despite our fear, our exhaustion took over and we both drifted off into a light and dreamless sleep.

When I woke up, the scene around me made no sense. I looked up and saw the blue sky behind the tree branches above me. I was at the bottom of a shallow hole, and couldn't move, my hands were bound behind my back. The cold earth was moist against my back.

I looked up and saw a face behind a mask and face shield, looking down at me, standing on the ground above the hole I was in.

It was a man and he was mid-sentence, speaking to someone else, ignoring me as I woke up.

"-can't let it bother you. They were the ones who ignored the news, all the warnings. We even put up signs in town telling them not to come, that we didn't want them here. What else are we supposed to do? You saw what happened to Becky. You want that to happen to your nan? How many people do we need to lose?"

I closed my eyes, flinching with surprise as he poured cold dirt over me.

KKKRRRRRR SHH

"I know, I know, but it just doesn't feel right. I mean, it's one thing to kill someone, but burying them alive? That's just gruesome," the other voice said as it scooped up another shovelful of dirt and poured it over me, avoiding looking at my darting, terrified eyes.

KKKRRRRRR SHH

"We went over this at the meetin' last Tuesday, Rodney, remember? The good word says very espifically, No murderin'. Doesn't say nothin' about burying folks alive, now does it? In fact, if I remember c'rrectly, there was a certain story about a fellow named Jesus" he said Jesus like a folksy southern TV televangelist *JJJuhEESUS,* "who went and got buried 'live, and came out three days later, fine and dandy. Praise be."

"I know, I remember the pamphlet. But now that we're here doing it..." the younger man trailed off, "Just seems a bit wrong that's all," he said too quietly for the other to hear.

I was completely terrified. It's amazing how your mind begins to race and kicks into survival mode when you know you're going to die. I began thinking hard, grasping for anything that could get me out of this. My mouth was gagged so I couldn't try to talk my way out. My hands and feet were bound tightly with rope.

One thing I had going for me was that I had restrained enough mental patients at my job, I knew that ropes were not as foolproof as they seemed, no matter how tight the knots. So many times I had expertly restrained patients following a code white, coming back five minutes later to check on them, and finding them loose and running around the isolation room, banging their hands and head against the walls and plexiglass windows. None of the nurses were ever upset or blamed me, except the young new ones. After a couple years we all knew that some patients were "Houdini" and all knots were fallible.

I began to move my wrists around, bending the ropes and trying to create space.

KKKRRRRR SHH - KKKRRRRR SHH

By the time I was completely covered in dirt the ropes were loose enough that I could almost pull my thumb through. Breathing was becoming difficult and panic was starting to set in. My years of swimming classes and lifeguard training as a young man came back to me and I tried to control my breathing.

I heard the two men packing up their equipment and trudging off. I tried to control myself and wait as long as possible, knowing even if they had left they could be watching to make sure we didn't escape. It only took a few minutes to run out of air, so they wouldn't have to wait long to know for sure we were dead.

Eventually I had my hands free. My wrists were raw and bleeding from the friction of the ropes on my skin. I could hear Christine's muffled cries through her gag from her shallow grave, right next to mine. I waited a few more moments, and then could take it no longer. I had to get to the fresh air above, who knew how long it would take to dig my way out. It was possible I had already waited too long.

I began to wriggle my hands out from behind me and tried to dig at the loose ground above me. The grave was shallow so I knew I didn't have far to dig. The locals had depended too much on their ropes to hold me, but I was a *Houdini*.

I used every last ounce of muscle I had to burrow and push my way up through the loose dirt above me. I pulled my upper body out of the ground until I was partially out, waist deep in soil, before pulling my legs out with a mighty effort.

I realized with alarm that the soft and muffled noises from the grave next to mine were no longer audible. I scrambled over to the dirt pile next to mine, pulling fresh soil off in great mounds with my bloodied hands, a few fingernails had come off and ended up in the pile of dirt, glinting in the sun, bloody red as rubies.

After digging like mad for a minute or two, my fingers bumped up against something cold and hard. I looked closely and realized it was her forehead. I continued to dig around her face and managed to unearth her head. She didn't look like she was breathing.

I don't really remember the next few minutes, except for my sobbing and weeping, as I hastily pulled more dirt off her body, committing to doing CPR once I had her up and out of the dirt.

I finally got her onto the solid ground above the shallow grave and checked her pulse. It was there! Beating weakly, but it was there. I looked down her throat to check her airway. It was occluded with dirt. I reached in and pulled out a chunk of earth which had clumped together and gotten lodged at the base of her throat. I cleared the dirt around her nostrils away and saw she was breathing shallowly.

I tried a sternal rub, a quick maneuver used to check if someone can be brought back to consciousness through pain infliction. I rubbed hard with my knuckle against the boney prominence of her chest.

"Christine!" I tried not to raise my voice too loud, worried the locals might still be close.

She started to come to, moaning with her eyes closed. I told her not to make too much noise since they still might be nearby.

When Christine was awake enough, we made our way back over to the cottage. Our shallow graves had been dug at the end of the driveway, beside the outhouse.

Our car was surprisingly still intact and appeared unmolested. I couldn't understand why they hadn't taken it. I checked underneath and all around for booby traps, but didn't see anything. I told Christine I would start it, that she should wait a little ways away in case it was rigged to blow up or something. I wanted to get the hell out of there.

I started the car and waved to Christine to get in. We drove away, leaving our luggage and all of our belongings behind. I had only grabbed my wallet and cell phone from inside, dashing in quickly and full of fear that someone was hiding in the cabin – no one was.

We made our way out through the forest and away from the cabin, moving slowly, looking up ahead carefully at every turn to make sure there was no one waiting for us. Finally we made it to the hill at the end of the driveway. I drove up the hill slowly, beads of sweat pouring down my face, terrified of what might be waiting for us once we crested the hill and approached the gate to the cottage. Would they be waiting for us there?

As we crested the hill, I saw someone was in fact waiting for us. A man in a mask and face shield stood beside a black Volvo at the end of the driveway. He was waving a little white flag.

I stopped the car. He waved meekly and pulled up his shirt a bit, exposing his waistline. He spun around with his shirt pulled up like that, as if to say, *No weapons, I come in peace.*

"Is that the doctor from in town?" Christine asked.

"I think it is."

He began to walk over slowly with his hands up, waving his little white flag without much enthusiasm.

I decided it was pointless to reverse and try to get away. There was nowhere to go with a dead-end peninsula behind us and his Volvo blocking the way ahead. I worked with doctors and knew they took an oath not to harm others. I hoped that oath might protect us now.

He stood about six feet away from the passenger-side window, practicing appropriate social distancing, and waited for us to roll down our window to talk to him.

Christine rolled down her window a couple of inches.

"I knew those two idiots were too dumb to finish a job like that. The human body is more resilient than most people think, you know. Plus the ground is hard up here and those two are as lazy as they come, I had a pretty good feeling they wouldn't dig those graves even close to deep enough and you two would manage to find a way out. I hope you learned your lesson."

"You- You knew they were going to bury us alive and you didn't stop them!" I couldn't believe what I was hearing from this doctor. He hadn't done the job himself but he knew what was going on.

"There's no stopping a mob when they're in a frenzy, son. And that's what you two walked into here. Guess you don't read the news much. Didn't bother to look what was happening in the area you call your *second home;* as if there could ever be such a thing." His face was impossible to read behind his mask. "How's your leg feel today, by the way? Sore? Numb? We usually don't inject in the dorsogluteal any more, too risky, sciatic nerve right near there that can be seriously damaged. I was pretty tired last night, guess it slipped my mind."

"Was that even a rabies shot you gave me?" He shrugged and didn't say anything.

Up ahead, the Volvo moved out of the way. I hadn't noticed the other person in the car before. I stepped on the gas and started to drive away.

"Y'all don't come back now, ya hear!" I heard the doctor say in a fake hillbilly accent as we drove off.

As we passed the Volvo I saw the nurse from the night before was sitting behind the wheel. His wife, maybe?

We turned onto the road and drove quickly back to the highway, speeding past locals' houses with boarded up windows. Signs on the lawns were spray painted with various slogans we hadn't been able to make out or even notice on our way in the night before.

KEEP OUTSIDERS OUT!
NO ROOM FOR TOURISTS!
KEEP BLUE ZONES BLUE!

Those were the tamer ones. Then there were a contingent of more radical signs.

REVENGE FOR BECKY
MAKE THEM PAY
REPORT OUTSIDERS TO THE COMMITTEE FOR JUSTICE

We finally made it to the highway without seeing another car on the road. Our tires squealed as I pulled onto Highway 7, and sped off, west towards home.

I thought my pet squirrel had the Plague
Now I realize it's something far worse

I never pictured myself having a pet squirrel. I've had cats and dogs, birds and gerbils as pets ever since I was a little kid. For the last couple years though, I haven't had any animals in the house; not since my old cocker spaniel passed away.

Still, when I saw the baby squirrel lying in the grass on my way home from work, I had to stop to check it out. The little guy looked only a few weeks old, its fur barely grown in. It was shaking and squeaking and making sad little noises with its tiny mouth. He was just a few yards away in the grass. I couldn't understand where his mother could be. *Maybe she had been hit by a car,* I thought sadly to myself.

I picked the poor thing up in my bare hands and cradled its tiny body in my palms, careful not to crush it with my oversized mitts. I'm 6 foot 4 inches tall and have hands to match. At the hospital where I work extra-large gloves are essential – I rip right through the large-sized ones trying to put them on.

The little thing had been shivering when I picked it up but it settled down after a few minutes and fell asleep, its tiny breaths quick and its heartbeat fast and thready, beating so hard I could feel it through its back. I made the decision then that I needed to take it home and nurse it back to health.

I got back to my apartment and made a little house for it out of a shoebox. I put a towel inside and the tiny squirrel curled up immediately and went to sleep.

The next morning I had to figure out what to feed the thing, as its hungry squeaks and squeals woke me up with the rising sun.

With a quick check online I found out I could feed the tiny creature with goat milk and a couple other easily obtainable ingredients. I left him in his little box alone and went out to get supplies, feeling oddly guilty as I closed the door on its pitiful calls for its mother.

When I got home I found it asleep in the shoebox and it woke up to my voice. I poured the goat milk into a toy baby bottle that I had purchased and managed to nurse the baby squirrel with the bottle. It sucked greedily on the goat milk and made happy little burping noises and ran around a bit afterwards. I let it out on the floor of my apartment and it scurried around and dropped its little turds on my area rug with reckless abandon. It was pretty adorable.

I grew to love the little guy as he grew in my home and I nursed him back to health. I couldn't figure out what was wrong with him, though. He was always hungry and never seemed to be full, no matter how much I fed him. And he grew very quickly into the largest squirrel I had ever seen – nearly the size of a cat.

Whatever hormonal issues he had, I thought, it was didn't affect him that much, he'd still run around and liked to play with toys.

But something seemed off about him. He didn't look completely squirrel-like. He almost looked like a mutant. The differences between him and the rest of his kind only grew more obvious as he got bigger.

Then he began to develop little red marks all over his body. I googled the shape of them and found a nursery rhyme. One that I had heard many times as a child.

Ring around the rosey

pocket full of posies

ashes, ashes

we all fall down

But what did that have to do with a rash? I kept reading, growing more and more horrified.

I refused to believe my little pet squirrel could have Black Plague. *That's impossible*, I thought, the little bugger was cute as the dickens. *There's no way he could be carrying a disease that wiped out a third of Europe in the Middle Ages.* The good news was, the Internet said there was a cure for the bubonic plague.

So, I walked Mr. Peanutbutter down to the nearest veterinary clinic and told them my suspicions.

They were not particularly welcoming, but agreed to treat my pet squirrel on the condition that I left him with them and went to the nearest hospital to seek treatment, since I had most likely been exposed. No sense starting another pandemic, they said.

The hospital wasn't very welcoming either, when I told them my situation. I had already started developing ring-shaped rashes on my skin, as well. They forced me to call everyone I knew and worked with. My boss wasn't happy I had been coming in for my shifts and exposing people – but I explained I hadn't known until now. I told them I had just been trying to do the right thing, trying to save a poor dying baby squirrel.

When I was released from the hospital I went back to pick up Mr. Peanutbutter. The veterinary clinic was just about to open when I pulled up, so I waited in the parking lot.

I waited for a while and no one came to the front to open the door. I double checked the hours on their sign and tried the door handle. It wasn't locked so I went inside.

The first thing that stood out was the blood. It was everywhere. Covering the walls, floors, and ceiling, all over the lobby and behind the reception desk. I found myself walking through it, despite rational common sense that would normally tell a person to call the police, and not to walk into a crime scene. I had a terrible suspicion and couldn't stop. My brain felt funny and since the rings had begun to form on my skin, I had begun to lose all sense of self-preservation.

My shoes made gummy, sticky sounds as I stepped through puddles of dark, hemolyzed blood. I walked up to the counter on trembling legs and looked over it. There was no one there. Just more blood, and lots of it.

Proceeding carefully, I went back into the first examination room.

I opened the door and let out a choked whimper. There was no one in there, just more blood. Gallons and gallons of blood, still fresh. Still, no doctors, no veterinary techs, no pets or their owners. *What the hell had happened here?* A voice in my head whispered back that I knew what had happened here.

I scratched at the red circle on the back of my hand. A red splotch was at its center and it was intensely itchy. I couldn't stop scratching it suddenly and noticed blood was starting to leak out of it, and pus.

I went into the next examination room, and the next, and the next. Nothing but blood, blood, blood.

I heard a crash from the back room and found myself walking slowly towards the door that opened up to the kennels and workspaces at the back of the building.

I opened the door and stepped inside the large room. Cages were stacked to my right where animals were hiding, terrified, in the backs of their kennels. The dogs whimpered and the cats were silent. None of them dared to hiss or make a sound to agitate the large form lurking on the other end of the room.

The creature, which crouched over the human remains, was once my pet squirrel, Mr. Peanutbutter. But now, it was something much worse. It had grown quickly from all the food it had consumed. It was now over eight feet tall, and didn't resemble a squirrel very much at all.

It was eating noisily, tearing off pieces of flesh from a veterinarian. His face was gone and his gleaming skull protruded through gaps in the skin. His eyeballs had been ripped out, I noticed, and his feet and left arm were missing.

"Mr. Peanutbutter," I heard my voice saying, without thinking.

His head whipped around and I quickly realized this creature was no longer my friend. I tried to back up and reach for the door behind me but it was already too late.

It raced towards me, impossibly fast, its long sharp teeth bared and dripping blood as it lunged at my neck. It was covered in blood, and slippery.

I managed somehow to stop its face from biting my throat. It came at quite a cost.

My hand ended up in the thing's mouth, as I tried to push it away. Its sharp teeth bit into my hand and blood went everywhere as the thing bit down again and again, gnawing on me and taking off strips of flesh.

Its eyes were red and its face was pure hatred. Its long tongue lapped up blood like it was chocolate syrup dripping from an ice cream sundae.

The dogs and cats in their kennels were howling and barking and hissing now, cheering me on, my crazed mind thought. I wondered if the creature's long teeth could puncture metal bars.

I looked around desperately for a weapon, anything. There was a mechanical pencil on the desk next to me and I grabbed it with my free hand.

I plunged it into the Mr. Peanutbutter's eyeball and watched as black blood sprayed out and everywhere. The creature howled in fury and pain and increased its attack, swiping at my belly with its long and impossibly sharp claws.

I stabbed the pencil into its head again and again, trying to reach into the soft tissue of its brain through its ear, its nose, its eye socket, any opening I thought might allow me entry to the horrifying grey matter of my giant pet squirrel's mutated brain.

The black liquid poured out from the creature's wounds and mingled with mine, seeping into the holes in my hand where the bite marks were and planting its poison in my veins. I felt my blood turn ice cold. Still, I stabbed, and stabbed, and stabbed.

Eventually I noticed the thing wasn't moving anymore.

I felt a little bad, thinking back to all the good times I had before with my pal, my chum, my little baby squirrel I had found on the side of the road.

A kitten mewed from one of the cages.

I opened the latch and it crawled out and up onto my shoulder. It burrowed its tiny head into my neck and I enjoyed its warmth, so I kept it.

I walked out of there and went straight home, not telling anyone what happened.

I'm still trying to figure out what to name the little guy. Maybe "Sonic." I used to love that game. Plus he's really fast. Not to mention the rings which now cover him head-to-toe. He's growing too, and quickly...

I fell down a bottomless pit...
but that wasn't the worst part

"There's a big chasm out back behind the barn," my cousin Todd told me the first day of my visit, sitting on the back deck in a pair of finely aged Muskoka chairs. "We can go check it out after breakfast if you want."

"Yeah sure, sounds good," I said, catching myself pulling off flakes of peeling white paint from the armrest and stopping just after he had noticed.

Of course I knew about the chasm, it was all my mom had talked about when she had been attempting to convince me to go out west to visit my aunt and cousins. She had been out to see them by herself the year before.

At first my mom had hyped the cave as an attraction and then once I had been enticed and agreed to go it had all been about safety, safety, safety.

We wouldn't be allowed to go into the cave of course, since it was a straight vertical drop down into untold depths. Even trained cave explorers were banned from spelunking into the chasm following the unfortunate deaths of four cavers, who had gone in back in the Nineties and never returned. The rock was loose and crumbling, the experts had said causing the climbers' equipment failures and their subsequent deaths.

95

I knew we wouldn't be able to do much other than look, but I was still intrigued.

The pictures I had seen of the chasm, known locally as "The Pit" were truly amazing.

It looked like a portal straight to hell. A yawning abyss that gaped like a mouth in the middle of a rocky outcrop, and dropped off vertically like a giant well. If the cousins didn't live in the middle of nowhere they could have opened a roadside attraction stand and made a killing, that's how bizarre this thing looked.

The hole went down further than anyone had been able to record. Even before the deaths thirty years before, there was no record of anyone surviving who had gone down into the cave, since its unreliable walls were known to crumble and give way without warning.

As we sat at the table eating bacon and eggs, cooked by my uncle Glen, Todd told his father our plans for the day.

"So I guess you don't want to go out on the boat and pull up prawn traps and try to catch a few cod today, then?" He looked at me expectantly. I looked over at Todd and he kicked me under the table.

"Could we go with you next time instead? It sounds like fun but I really wanted to check out that Pit thing," I said, knowing that my uncle went out fishing almost every day without exception.

"Yeah, I guess it wouldn't hurt to leave you guys here while I pull up the traps. Mary, Steve? You want to come out there with me? I could actually use a hand, since I won't have this greenhorn out there to boss around," he said, shaking my head amiably with his hand, ruffling my hair as an uncle can only do when you're still not old enough to drive a car yet. I smoothed it back down and gave my cousin a mental high-five. We would have the place to ourselves for the day if my uncle could convince my brother and cousin Mary to go out and help with the traps.

"Oh man, I'm sorry Uncle Glen, but I'm really not feeling great. I don't know If I can handle going out on the boat right now," my brother Steve said. I hadn't noticed him looking unwell at all, I thought to myself, a little annoyed at the thought of their pseudo-supervision. They were four years older than us and so they thought they were *so much* more mature than us.

My uncle sighed and made a few dejected-sounding remarks but ultimately left the house in good spirits. We went down to the dock with him and I watched as my cousin untied the knots, which held the boat in place, with the practiced motions of an expert.

I looked on with admiration as he pushed the boat off into the water. My uncle waved goodbye and we headed back to the house.

After we had raided the kitchen cupboards, eating the last two apple-oat granola bars and a couple of over-ripe bananas, Todd brought me over to The Pit on the other end of the property and showed me its grandeur.

It was even more amazing in real life, and Todd seemed to have a great deal of respect for it.

"Keep away from the edge, the rocks have a tendency of falling away without warning," he said, keeping back further than I thought necessary.

I walked a bit closer and I saw him tense up. *What a wuss,* I thought, and walked up to the flimsy rope which encircled the chasm. A placard was mounted and I walked over to it, thinking it would give some information about the giant hole that we stood in front of, but instead it was a memorial to the deceased cavers who had never returned from their spelunking expedition into The Pit nearly thirty years before.

In Loving Memory, Let us never forget
Reynold Breinhold – March 1958- August 1990
Stephen Fox – September 1959 – August 1990
Jeremy Fox – October 1961 – August 1990
Kelly Richardson – September 1963 – August 1990

Beside the placard was a laminated black and white picture of The Pit from the 1990s. The chasm was about half the size of what it looked to be today, it had somehow grown considerably.

"Wow, so I guess that was 30 years ago this month that those people all died," I said, looking back at my cousin.

He had taken another step back, and now seemed almost comically far away from the hole. *For some reason I felt like I was suddenly too close now.*

The ground seemed to shake almost imperceptibly beneath my feet and his eyes widened as he looked past me.

CRIIIICKKKCRRRAckkckrkkck

The ground just in front of me suddenly fell away and a chunk the size of a manhole cover broke off and vanished into The Pit. I looked down and saw my feet were suddenly less than two feet from the edge, the safety rope suddenly seeming much less safe.

The subtle shaking stopped as quickly as it had started and I backed away from the edge toward my cousin. Something seemed wrong, very wrong about the whole situation. My cousin was trembling, clearly disturbed as well. I kept waiting for the sound of the giant rock that had fallen into the pit, waiting for the loud crash that would show with mathematical precision the depth of the cave. I waited for the crash to echo up from the depths of The Pit.

But it never came.

I looked down and a crack had grown beneath my feet, stretching out from the edge of The Pit, towards my cousin's house. I stepped away from it instinctively, subconsciously. *Step on a crack break your mother's back.*

My cousin grabbed my hand with his, wet and clammy, and pulled me, rougher than I thought necessary, away from the hole.

We ran back to the house and went inside, where he insisted on playing video games for the remainder of the day. By around 7pm, we were starting to wonder about Uncle Glen. He had been gone for almost ten hours. By now, Todd said, he was usually back for supper, unless he had stopped by a friend's place, which was always a possibility.

Todd called him up on the radio.

"Hey dad, you coming home soon? I'm hungry!"

"Hey, bud, sorry but I went over to Johnny's place and kinda lost track of time, now there's a storm rolling in and the water's looking pretty choppy. I might have to stay the night here if it doesn't clear up so-"

The radio cut out abruptly.

"Dad? You there?"

"Yeah, I'm here. Do you think-" the radio crackled and static buzzed *"-yourselves for dinner tonight?"*

"Yeah dad, we'll figure something out," The static was louder now. He hung up the handset.

We sat for a while and tried to figure out something to eat. Steve and Mary were nowhere to be seen, leaving us slightly concerned, but we knew they could take care of themselves.

I looked outside and saw dark black-grey clouds blowing in from the distance. I had never seen clouds that looked like those back home. They looked nasty and full of destruction. Thunder and lightning boomed and suddenly it was pouring rain outside. The back deck was almost instantly flooded and water dripped from a hole in the ceiling into a pot which had already been left beneath it for the purpose of catching its drops.

Tink!
Tink!
Tink!
Tink!

Steve and Mary came back later that night, stinking of weed smoke and hard alcohol, after we had settled on a dinner of KD and some marginally soft saltines we found open in the cupboard. My cousin assured me we were going grocery shopping in town the next day. My stomach rumbled but I politely told him I was actually really full and it was okay.

I went to bed hungry that night, and realized it was the first time in my life I had done so. I was surprised to find myself feeling sad for my cousin and guilty of the privileged life I had back home. It made me feel terrible thinking my cousin and his family lived like this all the time, on the verge of not having enough to eat.

I fell asleep fitfully, unable to get comfortable with the heavy sound of rain outside and the occasional unheralded clap of thunder. The ground seemed to shake with each crash of thunder outside, but I eventually drifted off into a deep sleep.

In my dream I was in a cave. The air was moist and it was difficult to see, almost pitch black except for a light far in the distance. Although I couldn't really see, I could feel my feet sticking to the ground, and I realized with alarm that I was stuck in midnight-black mud. I tried to move my feet and found that they came up with an effort. I pulled my feet up one after another and moved toward the light in the distance.

KKKKKKRRRRRRWWWKKKKKKUUHHH

A giant boulder broke off from above me and I dove out of the way, finding myself lying face-down in black mud. I was stuck, unable to move. I felt a rock under my left hand and closed a fist around it. With great effort I managed to claw a few inches out of the mud, and pulled my other arm out, grabbing the rock and climbing out of the mud, feeling it pulling at my legs as I stood up. I walked forward and eventually felt the ground harden a bit beneath my feet.

The light was closer now, and the mud less tenacious. I move forward with purpose, covered in black-caked-on mud and struggling to breathe as it covered my mouth, nose, and eyes. I tried to wipe it away but only ended up with more mud in my eyes.

As I got closer to the light I heard the sound of waves crashing and my feet were soon stumbling out onto a white sandy beach. It was a small cove, encircled by towering white cliffs, with jungle all around the entrance to the cave. It was beautiful.

The water was crystal clear and blue, the pool of water in the inlet was small, shaped like a rough circle about thirty feet across. I stood at the edge, covered in mud, thinking how good it will feel to be clean, and I stepped into the water.

As soon as my foot broke the surface of the water I knew something was wrong, but by then it was too late.

I fell, headfirst, waking up as I did so, and saw the ledge coming at me, fast. I woke up falling straight down into The Pit. I had been sleepwalking, of course, for the first time in my life, and had walked headfirst into a bottomless pit. Smart.

The wall of the pit sloped in a few feet down, just enough to break my fall so that I didn't die, as I tumbled and crashed down about 50 feet to a ledge, barely awake, and felt my jaw hit the ground. My arm instinctively reached out to brace for the fall, and my wrist flared in sharp pain as it took the brunt of the impact.

I woke up to the world spinning. My tongue tasted coppery and I realized my nose was bleeding, or maybe my mouth, or both. My arm was on fire and I couldn't move it very well, my wrist felt like it was sprained, but maybe not broken.

It took me a few minutes to regain my senses and I found that I could hear a voice. It was whispering urgently from what sounded like a great distance down below me. It took me another minute to remember where I was and why the voice sounded so far away and echoing.

"Hey! Hey you up there! Can you hear me? Hey!"

"Yeah I heryoui... yeah I can hear you," I said, gradually regaining some of my senses.

"Good," the voice whispered back, sounding relieved, *"glad to hear you're... all in one piece,"*

"I was, I must have been sleepwalking," I said, remembering how I had awoken just as my foot plunged into the cold ocean water in the cove of my dream, waking to find myself tumbling head over heels down into cave, the chasm, The Pit. My stomach lurched as I recalled the view of the rock shelf I landed on racing towards me as I fell. A moment later I found myself vomiting without warning. Clear bile dripped from my lips as I coughed and finished retching. I noticed suddenly the smell down in the pit was horrendous. It smelled like a sewer on a hot day, like a dead mouse in a hot cabin, left to decay for the summer, like rotted black potatoes, spoiled eggs, and rancid butter left out to rot under the radiator.

"THAT SMELL!" I said suddenly, unable to hold back, forgetting our tones had been whispers until this point. The walls above me shook suddenly and small stones fell down, hitting me hard on top of my head and neck. A big rock fell and struck my right shoulder causing a stab of sharp pain there. I bit my lip and sucked in air through my teeth, trying not to scream.

"Quiet," the voice insisted desperately. "This whole place could cave in at any second!"

I tried not to hyperventilate thinking about tons and tons of black rocks falling on me from above, pinning me down, trapping me in this place, *with this smell, forever.*

"My cousin," I whispered, *"He'll come looking for me, he'll get us out of here,"* I said, more to myself than to the man below me.

"Oh gooood," the voice below answered back, *"I have been down here for, I don't know, a long time it feels like. I can't tell how long anymore, I've lost track of time."*

My head was feeling foggy, full of pressure and heavy, but the world was slowly easing out of the sickening spin. My left eye was stinging suddenly and my forehead felt wet, my hair crusty when I reached up to touch it, and I realized my head was bleeding. I traced the line of a roughly three inch long gash above my eye, leading up to my temple. I tried to wipe the blood out of my eye but found that only made things worse.

I pulled off my T-shirt and ripped the sleeve off, fitting it over my head like a makeshift bandage. I used the rest of the shirt that seemed relatively clean to wipe the blood from my eye and face, blinking as my vision began to return. *Thank God for modesty,* I thought to myself. At home I always slept naked but I had kept my pants and T-shirt on tonight in case my cousin had to wake me up in the morning, to avoid any embarrassment should the sheets not completely conceal my dangly bits.

"Jordan! Joorrrdaaaannnn!"

I felt relief wash over me as I heard the calls of my cousin up above me. I was about to call back when I remembered the voice below and its warning. If we were too loud the whole chasm might cave in.

"DOWN HERE!" I whisper-yelled back up to the hole above.

I saw the shape of his head black out a portion of the sky above for an instant before retreating back out of sight.

"How the-" his voice sounded frightened and bewildered. "How did you get down there? Are you okay, man?"

"I think I'm okay, my head feels like it just got bashed in with a rock, which I guess it kinda was, but other than that I'm okay, I think. I'm not sure about the other guy down here though," I whispered up to him.

"By the way don't talk too loud, the cave is- well, it's caving in I think."

"Shit," he said to himself, "I'm going for help, just stay where you are."

His voice calmed me a little bit. He would go for a rope and grab the neighbours or whatever passed for the equivalent of the fire department in this salt-water-swept corner of nowhere.

"Is he gone," the voice asked from below, "I mean, is he going to get help?"

"Yeah, we should be out of here soon," I said back.

"Listen, I need your help, my leg is pinned under a rock. I can wiggle it but I can't move it. I think the two of us, though. We could move it together."

For the first time I realized how hoarse the voice sounded, like the owner of it was dying or close to it. Back home I volunteered at a nursing home and had occasionally heard the voices of dying men before, the gurgling, strangled quality the voice had drove it home – we had to save him now or he wouldn't make it out. The only problem was, he was down there, and I was up here, on a ledge far above him.

"There's a ladder," he said, as if reading my mind. "I don't know how it got down here but I can see the outline of it leading up to you and I can feel it down here. I think it goes all the way up to where you are."

I reached down off the side of the narrow ledge and felt around for the ladder, thinking it was possible, if climbers had used this cave once, they could have left it as an escape route should their clasps and ropes fail on the crumbling rocks above.

I was about to give up when my pinky finger bumped up against something cold and wooden. I reached down further and felt the rough and splintering frame of a ladder.

"I've got it," I said down to him, *"I'm coming down."*

I was wiggling my rear end to the side of the ledge when I remembered my cousin would be back any second.

"I think I should wait for Todd, he might not be able to hear me from all the way down there," I said, not admitting to myself that I really was afraid, to dangle off the ledge and blindly feel for an old rickety ladder, to climb down to the bottom of a pitch black chasm where a voice was calling from, telling me it's alright, not to be afraid.

"It's not that," I whispered in reply, *"I just want him to know what's going on, that's all. Just hang on a minute, he'll be right back."*

"Pllleeaassssssse, it hurts, it hurts," the voice suddenly sounded more desperate than it had before, its tone now childish and insolent whereas before it had sounded confident, self-assured.

I didn't say anything back, trying to gauge the situation. My head felt foggy and I was having trouble thinking clearly. I didn't like the change in tone, but resolved I would attempt to help him as soon as my cousin came back. It felt important that I tell him.

The voice below made occasional pained noises but stayed otherwise silent for a while.

Finally, Todd's voice called down softly from above.

"Jordan! I'm back! I got a few people from across the way, we're gonna pull you out. We're tying the rope off up here then we'll send it down for you!"

"Okay," I called back up to him, *"I gotta help this other guy down here though, his leg is pinned under a rock, I got a ladder down here though that someone left, I'm gonna climb down and try to help him."*

There was no response for a few long moments except for the small rocks skipping and sliding down the sides of the cave above, raining down on me steadily now, pelting me with increasing frequency.

"Look, Jordan, you need to listen to me. There's no one else down there with you. Think about it for a minute, no one could survive that drop. I can't believe you're even alive but you are and we need to get you out of there. I think you- I know you hit your head and I think maybe you're a bit confused. Just, let us pull you out of there, okay? Don't try to go down further, there's nobody down there!"

I couldn't believe what I was hearing. Maybe I did hit my head but I knew what I was doing, I wasn't confused or hallucinating. I heard talk from above and words like *head trauma* and *concussion* featured prominently.

"I'm not crazy! There's someone down there, and he's gonna die if we don't help him!" I turned my head back

below me and called down to the voice below, *"Hey, just tell him your name or something so he'll believe me. If you're from around here he probably knows who you are, right?"*

"He doesn't know me, I would have been before his time.. I am. Older. "

"So what? Just call up there, tell him your name so he knows I'm not crazy. Or I'll do it if you're scared of a cave-in. What's your name?"

"I... I do not remember," the voice sounded defeated, as if it knew what I would do before I did it.

My cousin must have heard us talking and I thought for a minute he had decided there was a second person down below, his voice suddenly seemed regretful and apologetic.

"Okay, sorry I was wrong but let's get you out of there first then come back for the other guy, okay? One thing at a time, alright?"

"He's lying," the voice hissed at me from below. *"He will leave me here as they always do, you must help me, I'm, I'm bleeding, I'm trapped. I don't know how much longer I can survive like this. Minutes could mean my death, don't you understand?"*

I was tired of the debate. It didn't sound like the voice was that far down. I would help him myself, now, not later. I had only been down here for a couple of hours but that was long enough to know this was hell. The smell, the rocks falling down constantly onto you, the wet slime of mud that permeated everything and made it hard to breathe. This would be my penance for a few bad things I had done in my life, at least, the back-of-my-mind catholic guilt said subconsciously, even though we had quit the church years before.

"I'm going down for him," I said. more to myself than anyone else.

My cousin must have heard because he really lost it. If not for the threat of a cave-in I think he would have screamed at me. He settled for a halfway whisper-shout which resulted in a barrage of rocks falling on me from above.

"ARE YOU OUT OF YOUR MIND?? THERE'S NO ONE DOWN THERE! JUST STAY WHERE YOU ARE! YOU'RE GONNA GET YOURSELF KILLED!"

His words stung even more than the avalanche of rocks raining down on my bloodied face, but I steeled my resolve and swung my lower half off the ledge. A moment of panic set in as my foot searched blindly in the dark for the top rung of the ladder. Finally my foot settled on it and I found the next rung with my other foot, slowly and carefully making my way down into the complete blackness below.

Above me I heard people talking back and forth urgently. Clearly they had decided I was completely nuts and were coming up with contingency plans, since I wasn't exactly cooperating.

"I JUST NEED FIVE MINUTES, THAT'S IT!"

I continued down the strange ladder, feeling the odd
curvatures of it and wondering why and how anyone
would construct a ladder in such a fashion. The rungs
of the ladder felt ornately carved into shapes that each
felt unique, my fingers felt them with increasing
curiosity as I made my way down. The vertical bars of
the ladder felt strange too, and I ran my hand over the
face of it. It felt like.. letters. Only not from any
alphabet I had ever seen. The grooves were precise
though, and seemed to form the sharp angles and
curves unmistakably recognizable as letters of some
sort of alphabet. I tried to decipher them but the light
was too dim. I looked up and saw the hole that I had
fallen down looked tiny, the size of a quarter, now.
How long had I been climbing?

I began to notice that the ladder rungs felt much more
intricately sculpted as the ladder descended. In the
increasingly dim light I noticed they began to have
form and features and I realized at some point that each
rung was an oblong wood carving of a different
animal. This one felt like the wings of a bird and the
left side narrowed to the point of a beak, the other end
fanning out into tail feathers. The next had the large
flat teeth at one end and the unmistakable pancake tail
of a beaver at the other. An orca whale would be
followed by a bear, a squirrel by a hawk, with no
consistency or reasoning I could decipher.

"*So close,*" the voice said, very near now. Maybe only
ten feet below me. I was suddenly afraid. My hands

were shaking as I prepared to take the next rung of the ladder.

"*Whew, almost fell there*," I said, expecting the voice to be oh so pleased to see me. It was, but not for the reasons I had expected.

"YES! YES! YESSSSS! ALMOSSSST!"

I stopped suddenly. The voice didn't sound hurt or scared anymore. It just sounded *hungry*.

I had a moment of clarity where I realized what I was doing. This wasn't right. None of this felt right. I looked down and saw that my eyes had adjusted enough to see the vague shape and face of the being below. It was not a man, or a woman, although its features were distinctly feminine. Its skeletal form was long and slender, covered it ancient tattered rags that hung loosely from it. It was standing up to its calves in thick black mud that bubbled and looked alive. The creature smiled up at me with a mouth full of too many long sharp teeth.

Its ability to change its voice seemed to be a talent the creature possessed, along with its persuasiveness, I realized later. As I saw its true form I realized fully that I had been tricked, that the mental fog I had been feeling was the result of this powerful thing's grasp on me.

I looked ahead at the ladder and saw the rungs were much thicker now, and very ornate. They were no longer in the forms of animals I recognized, either, but strange humanoid monsters and winged chimeras. My throat caught and I struggled to swallow for a moment when I noticed the rungs currently holding me up appeared to be rotting, their delicate carvings falling away in pieces after years of exposure to the thick black mud covering the bottom of the pit.

I resolved to get out of there as quickly as possible, but felt for a moment as if my legs wouldn't move.

CRIICK CRAACK!

The ladder rung beneath my feet suddenly buckled, then snapped in half in an instant. I fell, breaking through several ladder rungs on my way down and smashing my face against a boulder as I hit the ground.

I struggled to maintain consciousness. My vision filled with bright mosaic spots and I felt for a moment as if I would pass out, but I fought hard not to, and struggled to my feet.

The thing was on me in an instant, its rotten black fingers clawing at me and snapping its razor-sharp needle-teeth inches from my face. I managed to push it away, the only thing saving me was my large frame and rudimentary knowledge of combat. I have never been a fighter. I fought that day, though, I fought for my life and pushed that bitch off me with all my might, sending her reeling backwards as she fell into the mud.

I tried to jump up and slipped instead, then had to scramble to get to my feet again. I looked and saw the creature was getting up as well. We had each gotten a few good shots in and I was bleeding profusely from a bite to my arm. The pain from the bite was spreading quickly with a dull ache that began to throb in time with my heartbeat. I saw ribbons of flesh hanging down and realized the thing had pulled my arm apart like a paper bag lunch filled with hamburger meat. Strips of loose flesh flapped around as I moved my arm and I felt bright fresh waves of pain, worse than anything I had ever felt in my life, as the adrenaline rush was no match for this degree of wound. I realized with dismay that I could no longer feel my thumb and index finger and they were hanging limply with no response to my brain's commands for movement.

The creature started towards me again, its black eyes shining in the dull light. I braced myself for its second attack, ready to fight for my life, trying not to lose hope. My chances of getting out of this place were seeming less and less likely.

As the creature got close, I lost my balance in the mud and slipped, falling to the ground. The mud seemed to have a life of its own, and it wanted to help the creature. I could feel it pulling me down like greedy hands and holding my wrists back behind me. I closed my eyes and screamed as the creature bore down on me The last image I remember of it coming at me, its sharp fangs were just visible in the dull light, already bloodied from its previous appetizer of forearm tar-tar.

I waited for the impact but it didn't come. I opened my eyes and saw an image that didn't make sense. My uncle Glen was hanging from a rope and punching the demon creature in the face hard. The mud momentarily loosened its grip, as if in surprise, and I pulled away from it, freeing my hands.

"Uncle Glen!" I yelled, impossibly, unimaginably relieved.

"Hey, kid, I'm gonna get you out of here," he said, pushing the thing off into the wall on the other side of the cave. The years of pulling up prawn traps and wrestling ling cod had given him a strength I had never appreciated before this moment. "What the hell is that thing?!"

He pulled me up out of the mud as if I was a child and took the harness off that was around his waist and put it around me quickly. He pulled twice on the rope as a signal to the people up above and I suddenly felt myself being pulled up, out of the pit. The mud-hands pulled at my ankles and feet, and I felt as if I would be pulled in half for a moment.

With a final forceful pull on the rope, I was lifted out of the mud, and up away from the bottom of the pit. I looked down and saw the thing was on my uncle, clawing at him with renewed vigor. I heard his cries of anguish and pain and felt immediately guilty.

The creature tore at his face with its claws, exposing tendons and muscles beneath. It snapped its teeth and finally landed a bite on my uncle's hand as he held it out to defend himself. I watched as the thing bit and tore at his flesh and then it had him on the ground, where the mud-hands enveloped him as he screamed.

He had come down here to save me, because I hadn't listened, and now he was going to die down here.

"Grab onto my legs Uncle Glen! It's your only chance!" I screamed, no longer thinking about the instability of the crumbling walls all around us.

He looked up at me and shook his head. I was too far up already, of course, out of his reach. I screamed up at the people above me to stop but they continued to pull me up, thinking I was simply being difficult. I watched as he tried with everything he had to fight the thing off, but the mud was all over him now, covering him except for his belly, where the creature began to feed, burrowing into his stomach with its sharp teeth. Gradually, thankfully, they faded away into blackness as I rose up into the light above. Rocks were falling all around now, and a larger one fell directly onto my forehead, knocking me unconscious.

When I woke up, I was in the hospital. My arm had been amputated above the elbow and I was delirious for a few days, but started to come out of it after my mom flew in from back home and I woke up with her frowning at me. Everything came back to me in an instant, like in a movie where the character has amnesia; it really was like that.

I didn't sleep for three days after remembering what had happened. I screamed and screamed and they had to sedate me with countless needles and I had visits from various psychiatrists and their young bright-eyed residents. They asked me questions which I refused to answer, until eventually they became annoyed and stopped coming around as much. I was discharged after weeks of care in the hospital and countless hours of physiotherapy and OT which helped me begin to learn to live without my arm.

Of course, it didn't take me long to realize that everyone was furious with me. Even though they understood I had a head injury before crawling down into the depths of the pit, no one seemed to really care. I had pretty much caused the death of my uncle, who had given up his life to save me. News outlets in the area reporting on the story couldn't name me personally, since I was a minor, but the stories written about the incident were not kind when it came to descriptions of me and my actions that day. My mom refused to let me give my side of the story, and in retrospect I'm glad. I would have just been called crazy as well as an asshole. Anyone who took one look at me in those days would have called for my involuntary committal; I was constantly shaking and twitching, looking over my shoulders and scratching an itch on an arm that no longer existed. My hair grew long and I stopped shaving. I stopped eating the food the hospital sent me at one point, thinking there was something wrong with it for some reason, it just didn't taste right. It tasted like mud.

The cave-in had made any chance of rescue futile. I had been lucky to make it out at all, I was told later, as an avalanche of rocks had caused a collapse inside of the cavern immediately after I had made it out.

My cousin Todd will no longer speak to me, and I can understand why. I'm not upset. The rest of my family is pissed off as well, obviously, but they're gradually starting to tolerate my presence again, although I can tell my mom will probably never truly forgive me for her brother's death. She walks around the house with no expression on her face. *A flat affect,* as it's called in the psychiatric field. I have been told I have this lack of emotion permanently etched on my face now as well. I hadn't noticed.

I haven't looked in the mirror for a long, long time. I'm afraid to look into any reflective surface. I try to cover up the mirrors in the house but my mom uncovers them. I've been told to stop but I can't help it. Every time I see a mirror I think of that water in my dream, my foot breaking the surface, and falling down into the pit, spinning sickeningly head-over-heels, seeing the rock shelf racing up at me.

Mirrors at night are even worse. They just look like that midnight-black mud to me now. I keep a bottle by the bed to pee in at night so I don't have to go into the bathroom and walk past the mirror in there. If I have to go number two I hold it until morning, no matter how sick it makes me feel.

The therapist told me I should write this all down, so that's why I'm doing this. She keeps asking me the same questions over and over, as if waiting for me to slip up and change my story, to reveal that this is all truly a lie, and maybe start to make some progress in our sessions.

Guilt-free zone my ass. *This is the truth. This is what happened. I remember everything.*

119

No Sleep Tonight / Jordan Grupe

Help! I'm trapped in a VR horror creation!

I'm a video game designer, and we'd been working day and night on our newest Virtual Reality game.

It's not like we got paid overtime, either. We were all salaried employees and it was in our contracts that we had to work as many hours as necessary to produce each game by its deadline – within federal legal limits, of course. Although most of us pushed it even further than that to appease the demands of our boss.

The newest title we'd been working on was a horror game. We were working on a next-generation VR version, which was coming along well. The game was in its final stages, with just a few glitches to work out here and there. We were in charge of adapting it to VR for a major gaming company's virtual reality platform.

Past versions of the game had been scary, but the version we were working on was going to give people heart attacks. I mean that literally and I had expressed my concerns to management. They were considering toning it down, but it kept getting worse and worse every time I tested it. And by worse I mean better, scarier, since that's what we were going for.

The game was meant to terrify. It had a way of drawing you back into it also, making you want to play more and more, as all great games do.

121

Our head of development, Garrett, was a genius. He'd been working day and night, making the rest of our efforts look minuscule in comparison. Sometimes I would spend a week working on something and would show it to him and he would tell me he had already made the thing himself, in a matter of hours, several days before. It could be infuriating.

Garrett was also a bit of a weirdo. Occult imagery and objects were displayed all throughout his office. He dressed like a middle-aged Goth – wearing black and white make-up, dark clothing, and nail polish. He would brag about snuff films and cult ritual videos he had found on the dark web.

Conversations with Garrett would always shift quickly towards the macabre, and awkward silences would occur regularly. To call him eccentric was an understatement. He was also a savant, and could code, model, texture, rig, script, animate, light, and composite masterfully – a set of skills rarely possessed by a single person.

He had told me cryptically that this game would be "very special to him" and invited me to his office for a private run-through of the finished product. He had done the final coding himself and told me he was very proud of the results. I couldn't wait to see what he had done since he had spent the last week in his office alone, barely sleeping. No one disturbed him when he was in the zone. At the rate he worked, I imagined he had made tremendous improvements. I was a little frightened for what I was about to experience.

We waited until after work. Sitting in his dimly lit office I looked out the window to see the sun had begun to go down and it was becoming dark out. The streetlights started to come on in the distance, flickering, and my stomach growled. I would be having a late dinner again tonight, it seemed.

Garrett finally came back from whatever he had been doing in the other room. I thought his eyes would look exhausted after the lack of sleep we had witnessed from him in the past week, but they were darting and alert. He looked manic, almost paranoid.

He quickly brought the VR headset over to me and tried to thrust it onto my head without a word, his eyes wide and staring ahead blankly. I stopped him, "Whoa, easy man! I'll put it on. What's up with you? You're acting even weirder than usual." He looked like he broke out of a trance and finally made eye contact with me.

He paused, looking confused like he had forgotten where he was for a moment, then laughed awkwardly and said he was just really excited for me to try the new update. He told me that he trusted my opinion. I never bullshitted him when I thought something was below his standards, which he respected.

I put the headset on. It was a helmet that connected with the haptic suit I was wearing. The expensive suit gave little shocks and jolts to make the VR experience more realistic. It wouldn't hurt you, but if you were getting shot repeatedly with a gun, for instance, it would make you uncomfortable.

I heard an unfamiliar click as he adjusted the helmet and pulled it tighter onto my head. I heard a high pitched whirring sound like a dentist drill and felt a pinch, almost like a bee sting, in the back of my skull.

"Ow! What the hell was that!?" I yelled at him. We were not off to a good start. That had really hurt.

"Sorry, new hardware, still getting the bugs out," he mumbled. It had stung badly and the pain lingered back there like a dull ache. It reminded me again of a dentist's drill, and the soreness afterwards.

"You turned the haptics down, right?" I asked him. He had a tendency to forget that step, and his simulations always pressed the technology to its limits. I didn't want to go home with bruises again like I had after playing the martial arts fighting game he had me test last year.

"Yeah, don't worry," he said dismissively. I heard him quickly typing commands on his computer.

An old wooden door suddenly appeared in front of my eyes and I opened the rusty latch, stepping inside. I brushed spider webs out of the way with my hands, feeling their softness give way as my haptic gloves swiped through them. They clung to me as I walked forward, feeling sticky and gross. Nice touch, I thought. Walking forward I saw that it was very dark in the dungeon, even near the entrance.

"How do I pull out the flashlight? I can't see."

"I got rid of it, check it out. I think this is better." He told me what to do and I performed the sequence of motions to pull out a match and light it. I saw it was burning down quickly, like a real match.

"Seriously!?" I laughed, "As if this game isn't creepy enough, now I've just got a match to see with. Let me guess, if I pull out a weapon the light will go out, right?"

"Of course," he said, "You can't hold a lit match and pull out a knife at the same time. Where's the realism in that? It would blow out."

I walked forward with the lit match guttering in my fingers. I held up my other hand, cupping the flame to block the draft. The darkness enveloped me and I was afraid as I stepped past each alcove where something could be hiding, waiting to jump out at me from the shadows. The match was already burning close to my fingertips, and I adjusted my grip to make more room for the flame.

I stepped quietly down the stairs and into the dungeon. I couldn't help but marvel at the realism of the graphics. The supercomputer we had running the game made it look like real life, and the movements of my avatar were smooth and seamless. The lighting and shadows were perfect and I quickly forgot I was playing a game.

Once I reached the bottom of the stairs, the flame burnt down to the bottom of the match, singeing my fingers, causing me to yelp in pain. I was suddenly bathed in darkness.

"Hey, man! C'mon, I told you to turn the haptics down, didn't you hear me?"

"Sorry, just did." Garrett didn't sound too concerned. It had really hurt and I told him he better turn it down a lot, it was too much for even the most hard-core gamer. My fingers were still stinging and it felt like he had done real damage. "I sure as hell hope so, that felt like it actually burnt my fingers."

I lit another match and the light flared up to reveal a tall dead man looming over me. He was dressed in a torn blue suit and was his face was falling apart, decomposing. Through the holes in his flesh I could see muscle, exposed bone, and maggots squirming. I could actually smell his rotting flesh, but that wasn't possible, was it? His mouth hung open as he staggered towards me and drool poured from it.

"Fuck!" I screamed, jumping backwards. He was coming at me fast and I felt my heart begin to pound. It was just a game, but after what the match had done to my finger, I was worried what this might feel like. I imagined the thing tearing into my flesh and ripping my belly open to feed on my innards and worried about the haptic settings again.

I kicked upwards, and my foot should have connected squarely with the creature's jaw, but he ducked, sidestepping out of the way at the last second with an effortless head movement resembling a professional boxer. He darted towards me with inhuman speed, his hands outstretched, jagged talon fingernails stopping inches from my face. I had the thing by the throat and was holding it back with all my strength. It was snapping its teeth so close to my face I could smell its horrible stinking breath. But how was that possible?

I gouged out the thing's eyes with my thumbs and felt two satisfying pops, which sprayed my face with blood and intraocular fluids.

"How am I smelling things in here? How the hell is that possible, Garrett?" He snickered and just said it was an upgrade he had been tinkering with. He asked how I liked it.

"It's disgusting, man. Just like the haptics, I get where you're coming from but you've got it cranked up to eleven! You need to dial it back, I can't take much more of this!" I felt like I was being pushed to my limits but found I still had a smile on my face, despite the pain and discomfort. I was pouring sweat and felt exhausted already, and I had only faced one bad guy.

The whole place stank. Garrett told me I should move on if I wanted to get away from it, and go deeper into the game.

"Go in a bit further, I think you'll like what I've done with the place," he said in a quiet monotone, typing more commands on his keyboard. There were lanterns down here so at least I didn't have to contend with the darkness.

I continued down into the dungeon and found myself killing baby spiders, pinching them between my fingers as I walked. There were thousands of them down here and they were crawling all over me, biting me with sharp little teeth. I crushed them as I proceeded, listening to their bodies pop beneath my feet as I walked.

Pretty soon I found myself in another large room, this one filled with dull light and spider webs. Oh shit, I thought. I've been killing spider babies and now here comes the mama. I spotted a knife on the ground and picked it up, grateful to finally have a weapon.

I heard movement from behind me and spun around to see the form of an enormous black spider. The thing was as big as a grizzly bear and was furry like a tarantula. Its many red eyes glowed as it skittered towards me on its impossibly long legs. Dozens of smaller, dog-sized spiders were coming at me as well, from all angles.

I slashed my knife in the direction of the giant spider's eyes and managed to catch it off guard as it was coming at me. It swiped at me and knocked me down with a giant leg. It began making howling arachnid noises. Green blood squirted from the wound I had made. Where the green blood landed it hissed and burned holes in the rocks, like a low pH acid.

The dog-spiders attacked now, their sharp teeth taking bites out of me as I kicked and screamed. I hacked with the knife and swung wildly, killing several of them and wounding others.

The enormous spider was on me again now, gnashing its massive teeth at me and holding me down as I fought with everything I had. Its mandibles raked my chest and I felt warmth spread across the front of my torso.

The green blood from the spiders, which covered my hands began to sizzle and burn, and I screamed. I was no longer screaming at Garrett, though, I had forgotten he was even there. I was locked in.

I managed to kill the spiders, but their blood had done a number on me. My face felt lumpy and I saw boils were forming on my hands and arms where the acid had burnt my skin. The flesh was red and inflamed, and pus was already leaking from several ruptured blisters.

I was panting and covered in sweat. The light from a tunnel ahead beckoned me further. My exhaustion was secondary to seeing what lay ahead. I continued on, forgetting that anything had ever existed before this. My life was the game and the game was my life. There was nothing else.

I saw another dim light coming from up ahead. I walked forward and turned a corner going deeper into the caverns. I had to reach the lowest level of the dungeon, there would be something waiting for me there. What, I wasn't sure. The idea nagged at me and lured me forward as each time I was plunged into darkness, there would be a light just up ahead, beckoning me onwards.

Occasionally I would have to pull the matches out and strike one, and inevitably there would be a creature lurking nearby in the shadows, about to attack.

I killed countless zombies, vampires, ghouls, and giant spiders. I was bitten by werewolves and captured by necromancers, who put IVs in me and injected purple liquid into my veins, making me feel suddenly less than human.

A few times I broke down in panicked fits of exhausted madness, laughing and screaming and clutching my oddly shaped head.

I couldn't understand how I had ended up down here, in this dungeon of despair. When things would get so difficult I could no longer bear it, and I had a breakdown like that, I would find myself waking up with no memory of having falling asleep. I'd bolt upright terrified, astonished to find myself still alive.

I had no compulsion to eat or drink, and realize now that Garrett was keeping me alive with intravenous or a feeding tube, maybe.

I finally realized all this after how long? Weeks, maybe months? I had been in here so long I had explored to the outermost boundaries of Garrett's creation. I found a seam, a backdoor leading to this primitive work-station. I believe Garrett put it in here himself so he could spend more time in his creation and still access the outside world. He likely assumed I would never make it this far.

When I first saw it, the laptop looked so alien to me I actually shrank back from it, afraid. I wondered what the dungeon of despair had cooked up for me in this, its latest attack on my sanity.

But then I remembered – it all came flooding back as I looked at the familiar screen.

After screaming for several minutes in a panicked fit of rage, I tried to pull the helmet off my head, but found it hurt badly to even try. It was locked on tight and the more I struggled the more I realized it was actually imbedded into the back of my skull. I felt a long, thick needle was drilled into my head.

I've questioned whether the technology is doing something to my memories as well as my senses. The thoughts I have of my life before this are hazy and difficult to grasp.

I worry if I spend much more time in here I might never get out – I may never want to. I can't remember much of anything, the more I think of it.

There's a light up ahead. It just appeared from nothing. I should see what's up there, maybe it leads further into the dungeon...

I'll take a quick peek and then come right back here.

No Sleep Tonight / Jordan Grupe

Stumbling on a serial killer while camping

It was late at night and we were driving up to the family cottage when the first police car came up behind us on the highway. My wife didn't see it at first and she made a surprised noise before pulling over to the side of the two-lane country highway.

We slowly came to a stop on the gravel shoulder and the cop car sped past us, the airstream buffeting us to the side. It was going very fast, I thought, even for a cop car with its lights and siren on.

After a few moments my wife pulled back onto the road. It was odd to see a police car, or any vehicle for that matter, this late at night on Highway 7. It was 3:00 AM and that had been the first car we'd seen for a while.

After driving for a few more minutes, she exclaimed again and pulled over quickly. This time nearly a dozen police cars drove past. We watched them go in astonishment. What on earth would be going on to cause such a response?

We live in Canada so murders and gun crimes are fairly uncommon. My first thought was an arson or perhaps a drug bust, but that didn't seem right for the amount of cars and the time of night. The thought of a murderer on the loose didn't even cross my mind, *not at that time.*

We kept driving and she pulled over three more times to let police cars go by, each time more than a few cops sped past at high speeds.

All told, about 30 of the squad cars went by before we saw the last of them.

The stereo had nothing but static for the most part, and twitter was silent on the subject when I used the intermittent data service on my phone to check for police news in the area. It was a sparsely populated community so the local police department didn't even have a twitter account, I noticed.

By the time we got to the cottage we were both exhausted. Our family cabin is a long way off the beaten path. We're at the end of an isolated peninsula on a small lake. It takes thirty minutes of driving down treacherous back roads (some of which barely qualify as roads) to reach the quiet little shack. And that's after the four-hour drive on freeways and two-lane highways just to get into the area.

We pulled into the driveway, which was just a couple of tire tracks in the grass.

I got out of the car and swatted mosquitoes as I pulled out my phone and turned on the flashlight app. The lake was still and quiet, with only the sound of crickets and bullfrogs, and the odd coyote howl in the distance. It would be another couple of hours before the birds began to sing and the bass began to jump out of the water making unexpected splashing noises.

I went up the rickety wooden stairs to the front door and put the key in the lock, turning it with an effort, making a mental note to put a bit of lubricant on it before the end of the weekend.

Stepping inside, I balked as I felt cobwebs on my face and felt something crawling on the back of my neck. I yelped and brushed the thing off of me, feeling the spider bite the back of my neck before I could get to it with my hand. I made a pained noise and said a quick prayer to Jesus asking him to prevent infection and/or give me spider-man abilities.

I heard something move in the darkness of the cabin. We had mice so at first I dismissed it as that, but then took a second longer to process the sound. It had sounder larger than a mouse, whatever it was.

"Hello?" I called into the cabin, my voice betraying a slight quiver.

No one answered. I was worried momentarily that a raccoon had found its way in. It was possible, especially now that I noticed a draft coming from the back room. *Maybe a window had broken from a fallen tree branch, allowing wildlife inside*, I thought.

There was no electricity in the cabin, since I hadn't hooked up the marine battery to the inverter yet. I used the light on my phone as I walked in further, taking slow and tentative steps, my heart beating loud and fast in my ears. My mouth and throat felt dry and my stomach felt fluttery and strange.

135

"Hello?" I said again, still sensing another presence inside. Something with eyes, watching, waiting.

I proceeded past the bedroom door and almost pissed my pants when someone put their forearm around my neck, tightly, choking me. I felt a cold steel blade dig into the flesh below my ear and a sting as it prodded past the superficial skin, drawing blood. Warmth trickled down the side of my neck and turned cold in the chilly night air.

"Not a sound." The voice behind me was not asking. It was a raspy-sounding man, his smoker's voice totally devoid of emotion. "Not a sound or I will fucking kill you. Tell your bitch to come inside."

My wife came in, saying something about how tired she was, and then dropped what she was carrying and screamed. She stood frozen in the doorway, mosquitoes flying in past her, the car headlights making her into a silhouette, a caricature of a scared person. Her hands were up at the sides of her face and her legs shook. She tried to say something but stammered and stopped.

"I'm gonna take your car," the man said. "Give me the keys."

I looked at my wife, and tried to tell her to give the man the keys, but my voice didn't work.

Another person was in the room, I noticed suddenly. There was a young teenage girl in the shadows, behind the couch on the floor. She rocked back and forth silently in the darkness.

The knife dug further into my neck and I cried out in pain.

"The keys," he said again.

"They're in the car," my wife managed, her voice just above a whisper.

"Your phones," he said. *Again, not a question.* I handed my phone to him, my only source of light. There were flashlights scattered around the cabin but the batteries inside would be questionable at best. We would be left in utter blackness, without a car, but that was the least of our concerns at that moment.

My wife put her phone on the ground and kicked it over to him, after he told her to do so. He told her to move away from the door and she came inside and stood in the kitchen.

Now we were at an impasse. He would have to let me go if he wanted to take the girl with him, the one hiding in the corner. I felt a wave of sorrow for her, knowing the feeling of just one minute at the mercy of this terrible man. His voice was inhuman, monstrous.

He took the knife away from the side of my neck quickly and stabbed it into my thigh, up to the hilt. I screamed and fell to the floor, writhing in pain and rolling back and forth. The agony was so intense I couldn't catch my breath, and felt for a moment that I would lose consciousness.

I stayed awake, though, and felt fresh pain as the man reached down and pulled the knife out of my leg. Blood spurted high into the air and all over his face, drenching him in my blood.

He laughed and looked down at me, his face crimson red and dripping, except for the whites of his eyes and his smiling teeth. He wiped the blade of the knife off on his shirt, carefully, methodically. He didn't think about my wife, still behind him. He had called her my bitch, but he didn't know what a bad-ass bitch she really was.

My wife had been taking a lot of classes, since our run-in with the locals our last time up at the cottage. She wanted to be prepared if we ran into trouble again here and had become quite obsessed with self defense and jiu-jitsu in particular. She had previously obtained a purple belt in BJJ, but was now even more dedicated, quickly progressing to a black belt in record time.

She jumped up into the air and managed to get her right leg up over his arm, the one that held the knife. A flying arm-bar is a difficult maneuver to pull off, especially against a taller opponent, but she had been practicing like it was a full-time job. I had spent many nights as her practice dummy. She wrapped her arms around the man's wrist and yanked backwards with all her body strength. She had been working out, and managed to break his arm with a loud snap. I'm sure the adrenaline pumping through her veins helped maximize her torque, as I had never seen her so successful against a larger opponent. She had also caught him completely by surprise.

I heard more bones crack as she pulled back even further, not relenting at just one broken bone. The man screamed and howled as his ulna and radius broke in multiple places. His shoulder popped out of socket farther and farther.

I thought we had him beat, then. But just as he had been caught by surprise, so were we.

The girl who I thought was his prisoner suddenly appeared behind my wife and pulled her off the man, screaming and swiping at her. She had a knife as well, I saw with alarm. It was smaller but she had it gripped tightly in her fist. The light cast by my cell phone which lay haphazardly on the floor illuminated the scene at times but it was mostly shrouded by darkness. I couldn't see what was happening, as I held tight pressure on my wound. I pulled off my shirt and wrapped it around my leg as a tourniquet, trying to make a futile effort to ignore my blood loss and get up to help.

The man was no longer writhing on the floor. He had a furious look on his face and his arm hung limply at his side. I was suddenly terrified as I watched him get up to his knees shakily and try to stand. He fell once, face-planting with a loud smack into the wooden floor. It seemed not to affect him, though as he just got back up to one knee again.

Then I saw in the dim light what he was reaching for. His knife was laying on the floor, just out of reach. He was trying to crawl over to it. In the darkness I heard the two women fighting. It was starting to sound like my wife was getting the better of the younger girl, who was fighting like a wild-woman. She had been screaming and sticking her with the tiny knife again and again, but was beginning to lose steam and slow down, her arms suddenly heavy and tired.

My wife finally got a hold of her arm and twisted it backwards, dislocating the young girl's shoulder. She fell to the floor in a heap, holding her arm and making hurt animal-like noises.

The man was just about to reach the knife, I realized. I shouted to my wife and told her to look out. She saw, but just a moment too late. She was going to try and kick the man in the chin as he reached for the knife, but he saw her at the last second and pulled away. She slipped on the floor, which was slick with far too much blood, as her foot missed his face and the force of her kick lifted her off her feet.

My wife fell down hard on her back but didn't stay down for long. She got up covered in blood and tried to avoid the man as he slashed at her with the knife.

My wife backed up into the counter and felt around behind her for a weapon. She found one.

The man came at her and lunged. She side-stepped out of the way and he went past her, flying with all of his body weight into the kitchen counter.

He looked like he had the wind knocked out of him, and was stunned for a moment.

That was when my wife hit him in the back of the head with the cast iron frying pan. Hard.

He collapsed to the floor and the girl ran over to him, screaming at us.

I managed to get up to my knee and grabbed my phone. I held it in the girl's eyes, blinding her with the bright light. She covered her face and cursed at me, her voice pure rage. She cradled her arm, looking defiant despite her injuries.

I picked up the knife the man had been reaching for and managed to get up on one leg. I held onto the wall for support and told my wife we needed to go, now.

She agreed and we limped out of there together.

We got into the car and drove away, hearing the girl's insane voice from behind us, calling after us maniacally.

"We're gonna find you, y'know. Don't think you've won, because you ain't won shit! He's gonna wake up and guess what, he'll be coming for you next! You ain't beat us! YOU AIN'T SHIT YOU MOTHERFUCKERS! You're gonna fuckin' DIE! YOU ARE GONNA FUCKING DIE! YOU HEAR ME?!"

We found out the next day when we read the paper, just what had happened. The man was a serial killer and the girl was his brainwashed accomplice and under-aged protégé.

The authorities had found multiple bodies buried in his backyard and had initiated a manhunt for him. That's why all the cop cars had passed us on the highway as we drove up to the cottage.

It was just our luck he had picked our isolated cabin, at the end of a peninsula, far away from prying eyes. The chances were one in a million, conservatively. He had been hiding there for just a few hours when we stumbled upon him.

The worst part is, I know he's not dead. And he hasn't been caught. We called the police but the two managed to get away before they could get there. They are both trained hunters and survivalists, I've found out since, so they know how to get by in the wild.

I only hope the police manage to catch them before they can find us. I'm worried because I know there were a few things in the cabin that could have identified us. A camp fire permit which bore my mother's name hung from a board in the living room. The police say it wasn't there when they checked the cabin.

I've got a new security system and additional locks on my doors, but I don't know if we can prevent the inevitable. It might be time I started taking jiu-jitsu classes with my wife.

No Sleep Tonight / Jordan Grupe

This is not a healing pool

I live near a healing spring. It's world-famous. You may have heard of it. Then again, maybe not.

It's a well-known tourist trap about half an hour away from my house by car, so I can go there any time I like. Others have spent their entire lives saving up, dreaming of going there, hoping to heal their terminal illness or broken body after hearing a story on the news or from a website.

And it works! Not all the time, of course. But every once in a while, someone steps into the little lake and comes out completely healed. X-rays and CAT scans, MRIs and ultrasounds, all confirm the impossible.

The doctors will even tell them: "This is a miracle." The Church is notified and it gets put in writing that a person was supernaturally healed. These documented events are extremely rare. Each miracle is closely followed-up on and if the healing isn't permanent it's no longer considered a miracle. But that's never happened to my knowledge. Whatever goes on down there, under the murky mineral water, it sticks.

The thing is, I've always been suspicious of the world-famous healing spring. The Church is so secretive about it, they refuse to allow any scientific experiments to be done on the water or the soil there. This despite the fact that everything from cancer to MS to bone degeneration have been cured by the mystery water.

The Church has owned the land for centuries. I asked permission once to take some scuba gear into the water to run some tests and they refused vehemently. Even under supervision they won't allow any exploration.

Security guards patrol the shore and bags are inspected upon entering so there's no way to sneak my equipment in during the day when the place is open. But I thought of another way.

I suppose I should explain why I'm so curious. Why I don't just trust the priests when they say it's simply God healing the sick with his divine power. I believe that's possible, mind you, but that's not what's happening here.

When I was eight years old, we went to visit the healing spring with my uncle. He had suffered from Parkinson's disease for years and they thought perhaps he could be cured through the divine power of the pool.

His entire body was shaking when he stepped into the water with tentative, quivering strides. But when he emerged from the pale blue lake, he was a different man. As he swam into the deepest part of the water, I saw his head go under and his eyes widened in surprise. It looked like someone had grabbed him by the ankle and pulled him under. When he came back up he looked different.

He strode onto the beach on sturdy legs, his gait sure and purposeful. I saw him walk right up to my mother and look her dead in the eyes, his face slack and expressionless.

"I'm fixed," he had said with a total lack of joy or enthusiasm. "Let's get out of this place."

As he spoke I thought to myself, this man is not my uncle anymore. But of course my mom refused to believe it. She figured he was the same old Uncle Dan, only healed.

I told her that uncle Dan was in trouble. He was still at the bottom of the lake. This new man, the new Uncle Dan, said not to be silly, that he was standing right there in front of me. But when he spoke his eyes flashed with something evil and full of hate for me at having spoken. They flickered pale blue for a second, like a second eyelid blinking sideways, then back to brown. He winked at me and smiled, and I saw his tongue now looked far too big for his mouth. It was bunched up and folded over, crammed into his maw like dinner leftovers in a bowl too small to hold them all. His yellow smoke-stained teeth were now white as snow, and he grinned widely, showing them to me.

I tried to tell myself it was just my imagination, but I knew it was true. I was just lying to myself because I was scared. *Who am I kidding? I was fucking petrified.*

The new Uncle Dan was not a nice man. Whereas my old uncle had sung and joked and danced on his wobbly legs, this man was serious, mean, and quick to anger. If I dropped something or took too long to get him a drink (he was always thirsty now) he would turn bright red and scream at me in a deep and terrible voice.

"HURRY UP YOU LITTLE SHIT! WHAT THE FUCK IS TAKING YOUR STUPID ASS SO LONG?!" He would yell and scream and curse. He never joked anymore. Before that he always had a joke or two.

My mom stopped visiting him after a few months and then pretty soon they barely spoke. But she never admitted I had been right. She stubbornly insisted that this doppelganger, this imposter, was still her brother, he had to be.

I knew she was wrong. And worse yet I had a feeling, a very overwhelming inkling, that uncle Dan was still down at the bottom of that lake. It was like he was calling out to me for help from down there. If I could only find his body, I could prove the man wasn't really him, that he had simply stolen my uncle's life.

So one night when I was in my late twenties, full of pride and fearlessness, I made my way over to the property. I had all my gear. My flippers, wet-suit, air tank, regulator, hoses, a waterproof camera, flashlight, and everything else I needed. I had been preparing for years to do this.

I drove past the gated entrance a little ways and parked at the side of the road in the tall grass. I got out of my car and made my way through the forest towards the little lake.

The night sky was clear and cloudless. The full moon shone and lit my path as I walked through the brush.

I had to hide once or twice when I saw the flashlight beams of security guards patrolling the area, but kept moving again once they had passed by.

I slipped through the woods as quickly and quietly as I could, making my way towards the healing pool further within the property. The security guards were everywhere. Dozens of them. Why did they need such protection for a little lake, I wondered. It only convinced me further that something sinister was happening there.

After a few close calls, once nearly walking right into a guard and only barely avoiding detection, I reached the water's edge.

The surface was still and black, reflecting a mirror-image of the stars and moon above.

I saw something move in the water and then it disappeared a second later. Probably just a fish or a frog, I thought to myself.

I put on my equipment, still hiding at the edge of the forest next to the water. After a few moments of gathering my courage, I stepped into the inky black water. It was thick with minerals and difficult to see. I took out my flashlight and turned it on. The visibility was still poor, but slightly better now.

I kicked my legs and was propelled forward into the depths, my flippers making the work easy. I'm not sure exactly what I was expecting to find down there.

But I definitely wasn't expecting what I saw next. Those look like giant figs, I remember thinking to myself. Have you ever eaten a fig? You know when you cut one open and inside are all those little tiny alien-looking finger-hairs? Like cilia on a microscopic cell, but larger, they group together like a mouth in the middle. That's what I saw.

There were dozens of them and they dotted the floor of the lake. They opened up like flowers blooming as I approached and at the center of each large fig-mouth was a white bulb the size of a cantaloupe. They appeared to be plants growing on the bottom of the lake, but they were massive, over fifteen feet tall. I had never seen anything like them before in my life. They were purple and gold and moved as if they were alive.

As I got closer I saw strange vines as well, coiled like snakes at the base of each plant. I swam down to look and saw they were also moving around like snakes.

The white bulb at the center of the plant closest to me moved suddenly. I was far too close to it, I realized too late, my heart pounding with fear. The white round thing rotated downwards and I saw what looked like eyes staring at me from it. I couldn't pry my eyes away, despite my rising terror.

I looked closer and realized whose eyes they were. It was Uncle Dan, only his face was pale and bloated. His brown eyes were wide and afraid, just as they looked that day when he went under the water and disappeared, almost 20 years before.

149

His entire body was enveloped in the cilia of its mouth. He looked like he had been swallowed alive by the disgusting purple fig plant. The little finger-hairs moved around his head and wiggled around with sudden activity. They fluttered up and down and seemed to draw him back in as he struggled.

His head wriggled and squirmed and I saw he was still fighting to get free. He was alive. Nearly two decades later he was still alive. I saw his bloated face was covered in fibrous plant material, which made it impossible for him to scream or open his mouth. The plant was feeding him oxygen and nutrients, I realized. It was keeping him alive, but why?

I felt something wrapping itself around my ankle and I looked down with increasing fear. I was pulled down suddenly and saw a long vine had ensnared my leg like a Boa constrictor. *Not good. Not good at all!*

I saw it was pulling me in, towards the open mouth of one of the giant purple figs. This one looked younger and slightly smaller. I got the feeling when it got me in its clutches it would hold me in its terrifying mouth forever just like my uncle Dan and not only that but there would suddenly be a new me created, a meaner, thirstier me. My thoughts raced and I suddenly remembered my knife.

I managed to grab it as the vine dug deeper into my leg. I could feel it squeezing my bones and crushing my body tissues with its powerful grip.

I reached down and slashed at the vine with my blade, cutting shallow gashes into the tough skin of the thing. Its grip stayed firm and didn't relent. With increasing horror I realized it was wrapping itself even more tightly around my ankle and squeezing tighter and tighter. I began to feel pins and needles in my foot.

I reached down again and this time tried to saw with the blade, running my knife back and forth quickly and ineffectively as panic began to take hold of me. Fear swelled and grew within me as I saw the monstrous plant was very close now, its alien mouth opening and closing, the cilia moving around with anticipation as if the thing were licking its lips with hunger. This one did not have a white bulb at its center. It wanted *me* for that coveted place.

I sawed with the knife harder and quicker, my heart beating fast and heavy in my chest, loud enough I could hear it in my ears. The pain in my leg was incredible.

The thing felt like it was made of stone. I hacked and dug with the pointed tip of the blade and tried fruitlessly to gain purchase on the writhing tentacle. The knife slipped and skidded painfully into my skin, causing me to wince in sudden sharp pain of another variety.

Another vine came up and began to pull at my mask, trying to rip it off my face. I slashed and hacked with the knife and managed to cut off a piece of this thinner vine and it retreated, but several others began to approach from the depths. This was not going well.

The agony in my ankle and foot grew and grew until it went completely numb, as the pins and needles sensation went away to be replaced by a heavy pressure-pain. I pictured my foot turning increasingly darker shades of purple.

I was beyond desperate. The pain in my leg was worse than anything I'd ever thought possible and my hacking and sawing at the vine was making no progress.

I took a deep breath and began to saw at my own leg, rather than the tentacle that had ensnared it, making quick progress on the flesh below the kneecap. Compared to the vine my leg made for easy work. The knife cut through the skin and tendon like it was a tough steak.

The pain was terrible, but the idea of getting free was better, and I continued sawing, biting down on the regulator mouthpiece and trying desperately to keep breathing.

I reached bone and continued to saw with the serrated part of the blade. I was making tiny bits of progress and starting to become slightly hopeful when one of the vines pulled off my facemask and another yanked the regulator out of my mouth.

I managed to get one last good breath in before my air-source was pulled away. I held my breath and swung the knife wildly, trying to scare the tentacles off, then went back to my leg.

I was through the bone – finally! My hand continued to saw through the other side and I felt a huge weight drop off below me as my dismembered foot fell down to the depths.

Kicking with my one remaining leg, I swam up to the surface. The other vines brushed against me as I escaped but I managed to get away without any of them managing to grab onto me.

I got up to the surface of the water and took huge, gasping breaths of the fresh air. My leg screamed in agony and I struggled towards the beach.

When I got there, several security guards were waiting for me. I got the impression they had no idea what happened beneath the lake, at the bottom. They were simply hired goons.

Their faces regarded me with pity as I coughed up water from my lungs and screamed in pain.

"You lose your other leg?" one of them asked dully.

Luckily they felt bad for me and dialed 911 before calling their bosses.

I managed to escape from the place in the back of an ambulance and wound up in a nearby hospital on the Trauma Unit there. I was there for over three months.

After multiple surgeries they managed to make a stump that could be fitted for a prosthesis.

The nurses and doctors were amazing, giving me encouragement and support as I made my "Healing Journey" as they called it. I guess I shouldn't laugh, it really was a trip.

I worked with prosthetists and occupational therapists, physiotherapists and orthopedic surgeons, rehab specialists, and finally, finally, outpatient treatment clinics.

It was at one of my infrequent visits to one of these clinics recently that something happened, which prompted me to write this.

I was sitting on the steel table in the examination room, trying not to slide off and tumble down to the floor as the disposable paper covering slipped beneath me. The occupational therapist walked in with her student at her side. They regarded me for a moment and looked at their clipboard together, as one.

Their eyes looked up at me from the clipboard, two pairs together, at the same time. Their eyelids didn't close, but I saw them blink a second set of eyes, sideways. The irises flicked pale blue for just a second, and they smiled at me.

"What are you doing here?" the occupational therapist asked me. "Didn't you hear about the healing spring? It's very close. We can show you."

Her long tongue slipped out of her mouth as she spoke and she poked it back in. A thick purple and gold vine.

154

I'm pretty sure my barber is a serial killer

Few people understand how good a shave from a professional barber can be. It's a luxury, really.

You go in and they treat you like royalty. They tilt that comfy chair back, wash your face with warm water, then lather it up and pull out the straight razor.

I go to Sal the barber every once in a while. Not every day of course, that would be extravagant. But when I want to treat myself.

When the pandemic struck, I was pissed off that I wouldn't be allowed to go see Sal anymore. He wasn't too pleased either. He seemed downright furious. He said he was going to show those pigs in city hall. Strange thing for him to say, I thought at the time.

The weeks and months went on with no haircuts or shaves from Sal the barber. He wasn't furious anymore though, now he was okay with it, he said. He told me things would all work out for him.

The killings started a few weeks back. The police said the murders were committed with a bladed weapon – extremely sharp and fine. Like a straight razor.

It began with a couple of cops, a city councillor, then the mayor. Pretty soon it was obvious there was a serial killer on the loose, with very specific taste. People hid in their homes, afraid to go out at night.

I had a feeling I would be okay. The killer seemed to have an agenda. He was going after the folks who didn't want the economy reopened, didn't want haircuts and movie tickets being sold.

The killer didn't go after the libertarian politicians, the ones who were fine with opening everything back up again. Nobody else seemed to notice, but I did.

When the barbershops and hair salons were allowed to open back up again, I went to see Sal. I wasn't sure if I still wanted a haircut and a shave. I had some concerns to talk to him about.

When I got there he was already unfurling the apron for me, the straight razor gleaming on the counter beside him. He told me to have a seat, and said that he'd been waiting for me. Old habits die hard, I guess, and his friendly smile drew me in. He waved me in towards the barber's chair, pressing his hands down a little too hard on my shoulders as I sat down.

I wasn't about to share my concerns with him just then, as he swished the blade against his apron, sharpening its polished edge with a faraway look in his eyes.

He yanked my head back before I could say a word, and shoved a handful of shaving cream into my mouth, completely avoiding the rest of my upturned face. I tried to spit it out, but he covered my mouth with his hand and said, "shh," as he flung more of the white shaving cream into my eyes, blinding me.

He began to cut with his straight razor, as he pulled my head back by the hair. He laughed as I spit the stuff out into his face. I screamed, choking on what was left of it, then coughing and hacking. He sliced little cuts into my neck and face, quickly and expertly. They didn't start bleeding for a minute, that's how sharp his blade was.

As I was distracted by my lack of oxygen, he took a nearby jar of Barbicide and smashed it on my forehead. The blue disinfectant liquid inside stung my eyes and the new cuts on my face and neck flared with stinging pain. The world faded in and out of blackness as I numbly fought my hands from being tied to the chair. It was a futile effort.

"You didn't call once! Not once! The mayor, those cops, that city councillor, they were here all the time. But YOU! YOU! WERE SUPPOSED TO BE MY NUMBER ONE CUSTOMER!! " He screamed in my bloodied face from inches away, spittle flying.

I realized now what he'd been doing. Those politicians, the cops, the activists, who had been killed. They had all been telling people not to open things up publicly and then going to him for black market haircuts. I guessed that he had finally gotten sick of their hypocrisy.

I spat out blood and blue disinfectant, which wound up on the floor in an alien purple puddle. Sal looked at it and laughed. It was pretty funny so I chuckled too. The room was quiet for a few moments except for our laughter.

157

"It looks like a clown threw up!" I said, trying to go with the flow, maybe seeing if he would remember all the good times we had together.

He laughed and then laughed some more. His giggles got more and more high pitched. His face stayed glued to the puddle, but his eyes rolled back, and stared at me in a monstrous way. I was afraid to stop laughing so I kept it up, afraid of what would happen if I stopped. His voice rose from its high laughter just one octave higher and turned into a scream.

He finally remembered the straight razor in his hand. Something seemed to dawn on him. He undid the strap holding my right arm to the chair, then undid the left. I stood up and backed away on shaking legs. Was he just going to let me go?

"You've always been a good customer, Jayson. You always left a good tip for me. I can't kill such a great tipper. It would be doing the world a disservice." He shook his head, "Nobody ever tipped me like you did."

He began to howl with laughter again and although I oddly felt like joining him, the prospect of keeping my life seemed more useful at that moment.

"I won't tell anyone, I swear. Just please don't kill me or my family, okay? Please?" I said to him, my hand on the door. He regarded me somberly.

"Listen, Jayson. A barber knows his blade. And this blade might be thirsty for blood, but not for yours or your family's. You're all fantastic tippers, and I love you to death for it. I'll only kill the dirty fuckers who lie to everyone saying one thing and doing another, how's that?"

I said that would be fine.

"But here's one more thing. If I ever find out you lied to me, about anything. Or that your family lied to me or anyone else about anything, ever. I'll fucking kill the whole lot of ya, how bout that?" His eyes were wide open and wild. His hair was askew, his white apron covered in blood. The straight razor was still gripped tightly in his white-knuckled fist. He was breathing heavily and drool poured from his open mouth as he stared at me.

I tried not to argue, just nodded my head. I backed away slowly and went home. We left town that night with only what we could carry.

After a little while of hunting around, we found a new place to settle down. It's a small town and we keep to ourselves, trying not to be found by him.

But people have started being killed here too. First a couple cops, then a city councillor. They were all proponents of a slow, staged reopening. A careful, methodical approach. They were all murdered with a very sharp, very fine blade. Like a straight razor.

My sleepwalking wife has an ugly side

When you've been a hacker as long as I have, you learn to read between the lines when examining these leaked corporate emails. This one stood out for a number of reasons and I've decided to share it.

I've blocked out the names of the persons involved as well as the company name and product name to avoid legal trouble for myself, but if you're savvy and know what's happening out there in the world of negligent pharmaceutical companies, you should be able to guess who makes this product. They've been in trouble before. Do with this what you will.

To: *Redacted*- Lead Associate, Legal Affairs Division
From: *Redacted* - Manager, Client Relations
Subject: Case # 2398542 - *redacted* Potential somnambulism side effects and related legal action

Dear *Redacted*:
As per our discussion earlier today, I am forwarding the letter I received last Monday July 6th from a client who claims his wife suffered from episodes of "sleep walking" and other events which he believes are side effects from our medication, *redacted* TM.

Below is the letter in its original form. I will leave it up to you to decide if a settlement should be offered in an attempt to avoid any negative publicity, which would surely result from an extended court case. My recommendation would be to give him the amount he deems fair without negotiation. It goes without saying it would be best to avoid further public attention being brought to this issue given its sensitive and delicate nature.

Thank you for your time and discretion in dealing with this very unique and challenging situation.

Sincerely,
Redacted
Client Relations Manager
Redacted

Attached document:

To: *Redacted*, Client Relations Manager
From: *Redacted*
Subject: My wife is sleepwalking (and worse I fear) because of your company's medication

Hello,
My name is *redacted* and my wife, *redacted* is experiencing numerous unlisted side effects from your medication, *redacted*. She takes no other pills and your company's prescription medication is the only change to her normal daily routine.

For a bit of background, my wife had trouble sleeping for years. She began having trouble falling asleep about ten years ago and started staying awake later and later, watching TV on the couch in our living room until she eventually dozed off.

After that she began waking up earlier and earlier in the wee hours of the morning. Eventually she barely slept at all. She started nodding off during the day, in the middle of conversations. She almost fell asleep driving once and I had to tell her she should stop operating the vehicle until she could get her insomnia under control.

She tried numerous medications but nothing worked properly. Either it was ineffective and she wouldn't fall asleep, or it was too effective and she became a walking zombie the next day. After trying numerous combinations and alternatives, she gave up on everything and lost all hope. She became depressed and started losing bits and pieces of herself. She stopped eating. She stopped going outside and stopped enjoying life.

Then we saw the ad for your product on TV. "*redacted*, sleep easy," it said. Well, we figured it was worth a shot. I took her to the doctor's office the next day and convinced him to let her try it.

To be honest, I doubted it would work. But I was amazed when I woke up the morning after she took her first dose and found her lying in bed with me still, asleep for the first time in ages. She was snoring loudly and I didn't dare disturb her. She slept until noon and when she woke up, she said it was the best she had felt in a long time.

I even wrote a letter to you personally, if you recall, thanking you for your company's product. It changed our lives and we were more than thankful. We were over the moon.

Weeks and months went by and the medication did the trick every night. I'd wake up to go to the bathroom in the middle of the night occasionally and would find her sound asleep in bed next to me, sawing logs. Until one morning, she wasn't there.

It was 3 AM, or around that time, and I got up to urinate and she was nowhere to be found. I checked the whole house, the back yard, even the park down the street. I couldn't find her anywhere. The car was still in the driveway and I was frightened wondering where she could have gone.

Finally around 5:30 AM she returned, but she was not herself. She was sound asleep, walking with her eyes closed. She came into the house through the front door and went straight back to bed. She slept a few more hours and when she woke up she had no recollection of what had happened. Odd to say the least, but after discussing it with her and our doctor, we decided the benefits outweighed the risks and that she wanted to continue taking *redacted*.

We installed a new deadbolt on our front door which required a key to unlock from inside. I started locking the door and hiding the key so she couldn't make it outside and wouldn't hurt herself. I was uneasy about it but decided to keep an open mind. I knew this medication was changing her life for the better and she was finally sleeping properly.

A few more weeks went by and I noticed her sleepwalking once or twice but it was manageable enough, although somewhat creepy at times. If you've ever tried to talk to a sleepwalking person you'll know what I mean. She looked awake and I'd start talking to her and she would reply in a normal tone of voice but the words made no sense.

"Morning, hon," I'd say.

"The drowning octopus is using up all the butter," she'd say back.

Which was fine. I would not complain if it was just sleepwalking and sleep-talking in gibberish. But that's not the worst part.

The worst part was that she started finding her way outside again. Somehow she managed to find the key while sleepwalking and used it to get outside in the middle of the night. I woke up and found her gone, again.

She didn't come back until the sun was starting to come up. Again I had looked for her everywhere but couldn't find her.

This time was different though. When she came back in through the front door she was covered head-to-toe in blood. It was mostly dry but some was still wet and left red sticky tracks on the floor where she walked.

I was terrified when I saw all that blood. What the hell had she been doing? I wondered. I woke her up gently, afraid of her reaction when she saw the gore.

I managed to wake her up and when she saw all that blood she screamed and screamed. I was scared she was having a breakdown.

She had a terrible nightmare, she told me. She had been fighting an attacker without a face. A shadowy figure made of darkness, who lunged at her from the shadows without warning.

She said in her dream she had a knife. She fought the man off with it until finally he retreated, stumbling away with blood pouring from his wounds. A knife was missing from our kitchen, I noticed. A very large knife.

I hated to do it but I had to call the police. If there was someone out there hurt or dying after a run-in with my sleepwalking wife, they clearly needed help. I wouldn't have been able to live with myself if I hadn't at least tried to do the right thing. I imagined an old woman lying on a street corner, stabbed and slashed, on the verge of death (the supposed attacker from my wife's dream).

The police were next to useless. They asked a bunch of questions and decided (without even bothering to test the blood) that she had just murdered a possum or a raccoon. My wife was relieved so we didn't argue with them, just assumed they had some eyewitness account or other information they weren't telling us. We were scared of what could have happened, but quietly relieved at the police explanation. Perhaps that was all that had happened after all, we told each other.

Another week went by without incident, then it happened again, and again, and again.

The police weren't even interested in coming out to check after the first time. They just looked at the first lazy cop's notes and used the same excuse. Just murdering wild animals in your sleep, ma'am. Nothing to worry about. Go back to bed.

But they refused to acknowledge the possibility of something much more sinister happening. Our town had a lot of homeless folks, you see. And suddenly I was noticing there were fewer and fewer of them. For a while they were at nearly every stoplight downtown, panhandling. But soon enough I hardly saw any homeless. Those who were left appeared wide-eyed and full of fear.

My wife was always complaining about them coming up to the car and hassling us, but I knew she wasn't capable of... well, I won't say it but you know what I'm getting at. She's not a psychopath so I knew if she had done something it was surely not a conscious decision on her part.

One night I decided to try something.

I pretended to go to sleep next to her, but forced myself to stay awake.

When I heard her begin to snore, I got up quietly and made myself a coffee. I wanted to watch her make one of her sleepwalking trips on the town. I had to see. I had to know. Who the hell's blood was it going to be this time?

I drove downtown and parked the car when I saw a homeless man. There weren't many left to be honest, so I took a gamble and hoped I was right. Actually I was more hoping that I wasn't right and this was all a big misunderstanding. That seemed less and less likely every passing night, though.

The homeless man didn't see me as I sat watching him. I waited and waited. Almost fell asleep a few times but managed to keep my eyes open with several hard slaps to the face.

Finally I saw her. My wife was ambling up the street toward us. A giant butcher's cleaver was clenched in her fist. Her eyes appeared partially open, the whites exposed. She had that look I had seen before.

The man was asleep and didn't see her coming. I jumped out of the car and hurried over to him, shouting at him to wake up. He didn't.

My wife got there just before I could. She swung the cleaver and took off the top of the man's head with one motion. The heavy blade made a loud metallic clang as it hit the brick wall behind him and sparks flew. He sat there with his brain exposed and looked up at me. He gurgled and drooled and blood began to pour from his eyes. He collapsed to the sidewalk, still breathing but not for much longer. She hacked away at his limbs and severed them effortlessly from his body with quick, powerful swings of the cleaver.

"Honey! Wake up! Wake up!" I screamed at her. I was afraid to go near her with that look on her face. Her eyes were still half closed and all I could see were the whites peeking out from underneath. Drool poured from her open mouth and she turned and grinned at me. An evil, terrible grin.

"The parasites are flying away like milk jugs makes me happy-faced lemon cakes," she said, now covered in blood.

I took out my phone to call the police. She wasn't waking up and I was scared to go near her. She looked at me with her blank eyes as I took out the phone and began to dial. Her brow furrowed and she suddenly looked angry.

"Disease deer make me rumple flicker," she said, walking towards me. The bloody cleaver was gripped tightly in her hand. Her face was looking madder by the second and before I realized what she was doing she swung the blade and cut my hand holding the phone clean off at the wrist.

I screamed, terrified, as she swung it again, this time at my head.

I ran from her, clutching my wrist and watching as blood shot out of the place where my hand used to be.

I ran as fast as I could and looked back to see her fast on my heels, chasing me. She was gaining. Running quick as a wild animal as spittle flew from her mouth and she screamed nonsense at me.

"Flagging rut lumberjack fucks!" she screamed, and threw the blade at me clumsily.

I yelled out and fell down, wailing in pain as the blade hit the back of my leg. I writhed on the ground and looked up at her, horrified, as she stood over me.

She blankly looked down at me and brought her foot down onto my face, stomping it with her heel again and again until I blacked out.

I woke up in the hospital missing a hand and several other body parts. Nobody believed my story. Fucking nobody. They said I had a mental breakdown and had tried to kill myself after cutting off my hand. *I've already told you, the cops in this town aren't the brightest.* Personally, I think the cops were fine with the homeless going missing. Just one less problem for them to deal with. They were more than happy to take my wife's reasoning that I had gone insane. An overworked psychiatrist spent twenty minutes with me and agreed. Bunch of assholes.

My wife would no longer speak to me, saying I was trying to get rid of her. If I wasn't crazy, that was the only other reason I would make up such a ridiculous lie, she told me.

The homeless man's body was never found. She cleaned that up in her sleep as well, I suppose. Although no one would believe me when I told them that.

But you know the truth, don't you? You know what your drug does, I think. I've read the reports online. The ones that are quickly removed but reposted again and again. I know what you're hiding.

Get back to me soon so we can discuss my terms. You can reach me by telephone at the number below.

Redacted

I understand it's a lot of money, but I also know your company has deep pockets. If you decide to refuse, I will take this story to the press. Don't test me on that.

You've ruined my life, and I am more than happy to ruin yours. I can't sleep at night now thanks to your company and what you did to my wife.

All I can see when I close my eyes is the horrible events of that night. Her face a mask of anger and hate, only the whites of her eyes showing, while she screams and cuts off pieces from me.

Sleep easy, my ass.

No Sleep Tonight / Jordan Grupe

Mr. Gleam

The commercial for Mr. Gleam Cleaning Service had intrigued me. The jingle they ran always got stuck in my head and I'd catch myself singing it at work, in the car, and in the shower, seemingly against my will.

The price didn't hurt, either. Mr. Gleam cleaning service claimed to be half the cost of their competitors. I had shopped around and their ads were surprisingly true! I called them up and they said they'd come by the next day. My wife had been asking me to book a cleaner for months and I was going to surprise her with a sparkling clean home when she returned from work.

The old house we lived in had not had a thorough cleaning for years, decades maybe. We'd moved in and done the best we could, but even with the help of my mom and other ambitious family members, we could never make a dent on the grime, which was baked into the walls and baseboards after years of neglect.

The previous owner had been a hoarder, leaving piles of junk for us to clean up when they left. The basement was brimming with old shit that all looked completely worthless to me. I couldn't understand why anyone would keep broken 20-year-old as-seen-on-TV gadgets, obsolete electronics covered in battery acid, mildewed harlequin romance novels, and boxes of moth-eaten clothing.

The smell was the worst part. It was like the old grease trap of an abandoned burger place. The previous owners had clearly enjoyed deep-frying their food, leaving the walls yellow-orange with stains that wouldn't come off even with maximum effort. We had seemingly gotten a great deal on the place but found we would just be left paying the difference with our sweat and tears instead of cash.

If our house could look as pristine as the pictures on the Mr. Gleam website of satisfied customer homes, we would be in good shape. We wanted a fresh start before beginning to paint and start our renovation projects.

The crew had come to the door right on time, dressed in pale yellow jumpsuits. "Mr. Gleam" was embroidered on the neatly pressed uniforms as well as the image of Mr. Gleam, himself. The mascot for the company was a burly, bespectacled older man with a shining bald head. He proclaimed on the commercials, "We guarantee you'll be satisfied! Our team will have your place sparkling before you can say, 'Mr. Gleam!'"

The crew was all smiles and handshakes, overly friendly and attentive to detail as I showed them around the house. I was a bit embarrassed when we got down to the basement and to what we had begun to call "the dump". A pile of trash we had yet to make any progress on. I was apologizing, saying they needn't bother with this room, when I noticed a mouse running into the pile.

"Oh no! I'm so sorry, we've never seen mice down here before. I thought the exterminator got them all before we moved in. I guess they found a way in somewhere."

The man in the pale yellow jumpsuit didn't let the smile leave his face, even for a second. He marked a few notes on his clipboard, looking around the basement

"Don't worry! Mr. Gleam will take care of all this!" His reaction surprised me a bit. I thought maybe the guy had a few screws loose. His smile was way too wide and full of too many teeth. Didn't he realize they would be here all day and late into the night?

"We'll be done in an hour, two at the most. Why don't you go out and grab a coffee or some lunch and we'll call you when we're done. How's that sound?" The Joker's smile never left his face, though it didn't touch his eyes.

I had to admit it sounded fantastic to me. I couldn't believe they would be done so quickly but the reviews online had said the same – "The fastest clean, the brightest shine!" was how they advertised.

I figured they would bring in a few more people. The small group assembled didn't seem to be enough, especially to tackle this huge job. I knew they were pros, but this would be one for the record books. Unless he was overselling it, I thought.

"Okay, if you say so," I said dubiously. "Just give me a call on my cell when you're finished with everything."

As I pulled out of the driveway I thought about where I could go to kill some time. I decided to just grab a coffee and sit on the side street and wait for them to call. I had nothing better to do than watch Netflix on my phone, anyways, and I was curious. I wanted to spy on them a bit. This whole plan of theirs seemed impossible. The house wasn't small and there was a lot to do for such a tiny crew. If they finished in four or five hours and the house looked clean it would be a miracle in my mind.

I got back from grabbing a coffee just as the cleaners were unloading a very long black duffel bag from the van. At first I thought it was vacuum equipment, until I saw something was thrashing and kicking inside it.

Strange, I thought.

I watched them bring the long, long duffel inside through the garage. It looked very odd. The bag itself was like a clown car prank joke, it just kept coming and coming from the back of the van with no end in sight. A colorless handkerchief from a magician's pocket.

Finally they finished. The duffel must have been the only thing in the back of the van, I thought. It was so big there wouldn't have been room for much else. So where was the rest of the cleaning equipment? I wondered if they had another van parked somewhere, but it didn't look like it.

I waited until they were inside and quickly snuck around back. I had to see what the hell was in the freakishly long bag. It looked alive, whatever it was, moving around in there. But it could have been just a trick of the light or my eyes.

I got around back and looked in through the window, blocking the glare with my hands. I saw the cleaners unzipping the bag as they stood next to the pile of detritus in the basement.

They opened it and something long and dark began to emerge. A pair of long, hairy antennae probed around curiously. Its mandibles clicked and twitched and more and more legs came out of the bag. The long, lumpy body, which emerged looked like a millipede, but this one was longer than an anaconda and three times as wide. It skittered out of the bag on its many, many legs.

I looked in horror as it began to explore and then consume the waste in the pile. It fed ravenously, drool flying and pouring from its disgusting face. I saw a mouse try to scurry away but the thing snapped it up and crunched its tiny bones as it squeaked and squealed.

I looked at the workers in their yellow jumpsuits and saw their eyes no longer looked human. They glowed a faint light-blue.

The cleaners walked around, entranced, gathering what seemed to be the nastiest garbage they could find, old radios and electronics I had set aside for safety, since they were covered in battery acid, were snapped up like bon bons as the thing's mandibles crunched an old radio in half like a pretzel.

The giant black millipede gorged and feasted as I watched, hypnotized.

Eventually it began to slow down and it looked like it was becoming full, its impossibly long belly swollen and bloated.

I saw it lay down for a moment. It rolled over and large yellow eggs began to pour out of it. The things spilled all over the floor, rolling around like loose oranges. This went on until there were hundreds of eggs all over the floor, and the place looked like a jaundiced ball pit in a horror play-place.

The millipede began to gorge again. A large rat tried to scamper away but was snapped up and eaten like a palate cleanser for the next course.

I hadn't even known there were rats, but this thought hardly disgusted me as it normally would. Rats suddenly seemed quite tame and docile compared to this hideous demon-creature. Drool poured from its maw and I got a good look at its face for the first time. Its mouth was filled with rows and rows of teeth, going back all the way down its throat. Its eyes glowed the same pale blue as the workers.

Its mandibles clicked and chittered as it seemed to communicate with them. They looked at it with reverence and brought it offerings of moldy quilts, broken tennis rackets, and old shoes.

I began to hear the catchy jingle of their company theme song in my head, but now with different words. The right words, I thought.

Mr. Gleam, Mr. Gleam,

He will rend your flesh from bone

Mr. Gleam, Mr. Gleam,

You will scream and you will moan

I stood up, horrified, backing away from the window as I saw the yellow eggs begin to hatch. Hundreds of smaller millipedes emerged and began to roam around and feast on mice, bugs, and refuse.

I ran from the house and across the street to my car. I looked back and saw the cleaners were following after me and I started up my old shit-box as fast as I could and burnt rubber, fleeing with a terrified glance over my shoulder. They did not pursue. Who would believe my story, anyways?

Now the question remains – how do I explain this to my wife? How do I tell her that the house is now clean, spotless, in fact? But we can never, ever, go back there.

I met my doppelganger

Not long ago, I met a man on a street corner who looked exactly like me.

I had heard of doppelgangers before. I had even read a scientific article recently saying that there's someone out there who looks just like you, but chances are you'll never meet them. I figured mine was over in Germany somewhere, maybe, where my dad had been born. I'm tall with slightly Nordic features and light brown hair.

The man was my height, with the same face, same hair color, same body shape, and even his voice sounded like mine as he spoke to me, although all of these features on his part were weathered and worn.

"Change?" He implored, his cup held out.

The only things off about him were his hair and clothing. I shaved my head and face whereas this man had long hair down to his shoulders and a greasy beard flecked with premature whiteness. His clothing was also dirty and ripped in places. He sat on an old blanket with a traveller's backpack at his side. His hand trembled slightly as he offered the cup to me. He didn't look at my face.

"Sure," I said, and as he looked up his expression changed to a gleeful grin, which seemed too wide for his face. He had a greedy, manic look now, which struck me as odd. I dug around in my pocket and dropped the couple dollars I had into his cup. My good deed for the day, I thought.

He kept the weird, crooked grin on his face, and stared at me as I walked away. I didn't say it out loud but I could tell the man saw it too. We could have been twins, in another life. I reminded myself how fortunate I was to have the life that I did.

When I got home I told my Oma about it.

"It was really weird, the guy was like my identical twin," I said.

"Dein doppelganger," she said, laughing.

"Exactly!" I said. "Except this guy was obviously going through some really hard times. I gave him a couple bucks. I hope he spends it on food." I supposed if the man did spend it on booze or drugs I couldn't blame him, I would want an escape too if I was in his shoes.

"See, Yayson," she always said my name like this, pronouncing the "J" as a "Y", "das is vhy we must be grateful for vhat ve have." Her thick accent had never left her, even though she had come to Canada nearly 50 years ago, when she was in her twenties.

I agreed with her and told her I was just thinking the same thing, that it wasn't fair one person should be born to suffer and another to have a decent life. We were blessed, she said plainly.

I went to work the next day at the call center; it was a soul-crushing day, as always. The calls all blended together and at the end of it all I felt used up and exhausted. It was an outbound calling center with an auto dialer, so when you'd hang up from one call, the phone would already be ringing and sometimes the person on the other end picked up before you could, saying, "Hello? Hello?" angrily and impatiently.

You would be expected to move on from whatever furious customer whose dinner you had just interrupted and go straight into the script for the next call, trying to upsell them on their satellite TV service, or to collect on their overdue phone bill, or to encourage them to switch internet providers. And don't forget to smile!

"The customers can hear when you're smiling," we were told frequently by our overzealous educator. "And they can always tell if you're frowning. Keep a smile on your face all the time or they won't buy anything from you."

We handled multiple accounts and had to be able to switch between scripts on the fly. It was mentally exhausting. I spent a lot of time in the bathroom and refilling my water bottle, getting scolding looks from quality assurance people who would track me with their stopwatches.

When I finished work, I went into the break room to grab my bag and found that it was gone. I had hung it from a hook in the locked room and someone had stolen it. It contained my phone, wallet, and car keys. *Perfect!!*

I told the security guard and he said they would go back and look through the camera footage to try to find the person who did it. They also called the police for me when I went outside and found my car was gone. Taken by the same thief, no doubt.

After the police took a statement from me, I phoned my Oma to see if she could pay for a cab. There was no answer. Odd, I thought, since she rarely left the house without me. She was healthy but also a homebody.

I managed to borrow twenty dollars from a co-worker and told them I would pay them back the next day. They didn't look pleased about it, saying they really needed it back. I apologized humbly after thanking them repeatedly.

I took the cab home and when I got there the doors were locked. I waited on the front steps after knocking loudly on the door for ten minutes. My shift had ended at nine and I had been stuck there until midnight dealing with the police. I didn't have anyone to call to let me in except for my Oma. She was next to deaf without her heading aids and was probably asleep.

I decided to just sleep on the bench out on the porch, rather than wake up the whole neighbourhood banging on the door. It was a warm night and I knew my Oma was okay, she wasn't frail or in danger of falling, so I wasn't worried about that. I figured she must have gone to sleep, thinking I was pulling a double shift at work as I sometimes did.

The call center was open 24/7 and during the night we took inbound customer service calls for an internet service provider. It wasn't uncommon for someone to call in sick and occasionally they would offer time and a half to stay. I hated it but at least inbound calls overnight were few and far between. The call queue was sometimes empty and we would sit there for 20 minutes between calls, shooting the shit and playing hangman. I worked next to a guy, Cam, who was a "South Park" fanatic like me, so we would use obscure quotes from the show for the fill-in-the-blanks game, trying to stump each other, while we played volleyball with a detachable head from a "Kenny" plush toy. The atmosphere was quite chill overnight.

I woke up to blinding pain, the worst I had ever felt. It felt like my face was on fire! I tried to focus and come out of my dreams, startled, and realized someone was pressing their knee to my chest and holding a hot clothes iron to my mouth. I felt my flesh melting and dripping. I tried to scream but couldn't. I tried to push the dark figure off of me, its face covered in a black ski-mask, but it was too strong. It pushed me back down and used its body weight to hold me in place as the iron continued to melt my flesh, my mouth felt like it was suddenly glued together. The piercing brown eyes glaring back at me from the slit in the ski-mask were all too familiar as my own.

I passed out suddenly from the pain and when I woke up, the police were standing over me. I looked at my hand and saw the iron was gripped tightly by my own fist! It was still plugged in and glowing bright red. The deck beneath it was burnt, black and charred.

One police officer walked over calmly to the outlet and unplugged the iron. They were shaking their heads and looking at me disgustedly in the glow of the security lights. The moon and stars overhead indicated it was night, but I had no sense of time or place for a minute. I tried to sit up with an effort, and when I did, the police officer used his foot and pushed it into my chest, knocking me back down to the deck.

I tried to shout at him, scream at him, but I couldn't. My mouth wouldn't open. It was melted shut. I wanted to tell them what had happened, that I had been attacked, assaulted, almost killed! But they looked at me with disgust. I couldn't even imagine what my face looked like.

I looked down and saw my clothing was different than what I had fallen asleep in. It looked dirty and ripped, and I realized with increasing horror it was the same clothing of the homeless man I had seen on the street.

My suspicions were confirmed when the police led me roughly, handcuffed, to a cop car. My Oma was standing nearby, in the doppelganger's arms. He was now clean shaven and bald, and was consoling her. He looked up at me as he patted her on the back and smiled at me, just faintly. I couldn't help it; I lunged at him, trying to attack him even though the handcuffs were still clamped firmly shut, holding my wrists behind me. The police threw me to the ground and my face hit the pavement, hard. A fresh wave of agony made me feel faint again as the pain in my face flared angrily. The dirt and grit from the side of the road rubbed into my wounded mouth and I saw blood was everywhere when they finally pulled me to my feet.

The doppelganger was leading my Oma into the house, holding her close as she cried. She stumbled as she tried to walk with tears in her eyes. I heard him telling her it was okay, that I was mentally ill, that it was the same man from the street corner the other day, and the police would help me.

The cops threw me into the back of their cruiser. They brought me to the hospital where I was given treatment in the burn unit. I was seen by doctors for my wounds, then seen by different doctors for my brains. They put bandages on my burns, and told me to take some medication for my mind, to help with what they diagnosed as paranoid schizophrenia and psychosis.

They sent me to a hospital where I was told I would remain until the committee in charge of such things decided I was fit to be released. It depended on how much progress I made. Another patient told me he had been there for five years. He seemed perfectly sane to me.

He told me how he had been charged with a crime, and decided he would fake crazy to try to avoid prison. It had worked, and when he got there he realized he had made a mistake. His sentence would have been six months at the most, but after five years he was still there. He said it was a lot easier to convince people you're crazy than to convince them you're not.

I'm beginning to see what he means.

No Sleep Tonight / Jordan Grupe

My cat and I joined a local social club

My cat and I were best friends. I know, some people just say that, but we really were.

Not so much anymore.

She's a smart cat. Always was. She'd play fetch with a drinking straw, a game we'd play for hours on end until one of us would get bored. I had her trained to sit and wait before eating her dinner.

She'd sit there politely while I poured kibbles into her bowl, then she would look up at me expectantly with her big golden eyes. I'd say "okay" and she'd chow down.

She was always there for me to cheer me up when I was feeling down. She'd sense my sadness and climb up onto my chest and get all snuggly, nuzzling her head against my hand and purring. It was like she just knew how I was feeling and wanted to help somehow.

So I was worried when she started fretting at the back door the other night. She was pawing at the screen and making concerned little mewing sounds. Peebs was a sensitive little one.

"What's wrong, Peebs? You wanna go outside?"

She was allowed out in the back yard but didn't go out there much. She preferred to stay inside with me where it was warm and cozy. She wasn't one for chasing squirrels or birds. Usually she'd go out, eat some grass, roll around, and be back scratching at the door five minutes later.

I opened the door for her and held it open. She just stared at me. I tried to give her a little push but she planted her feet stubbornly. She looked out the door, looked at me. Looked out the door, looked at me again. Her way of saying, "I want you to come with me."

She waited for me to step outside then followed along quickly and passed by me.   She sprinted off ahead of me.

"Peebs, where you going?!" I called after her. She continued to run towards the back gate so I followed her, jogging, not yet all that concerned.

I got to the gate and noticed that someone had left it open. I shared the house with another renter who lived in the basement and he occasionally forgot to latch the gate. Peebs had gotten out once because of it and I had to tell him to be more careful. Looked like he would need another reminder.

Peebs was far ahead of me now, I saw her tiny footsteps moving forward in the orange glow of a streetlight. Her pitch-black body disappearing into the night a second later.

"Peebs!" I was getting really worried now. She had never done something like this before. I ran after her, as fast as I could, barely tracking her little black body running ahead of me off into the night.

My heart was beating faster now. I had lost sight of her. I continued running in the direction she had gone, hoping to catch a glimpse of her.

I finally saw her tail, just the end of it, as it disappeared behind a car in a driveway up ahead. The security lights lit up above the garage on the little bungalow. I caught up just in time to see her climbing under the gate into the back yard of the house. I looked around and realized it was Mr. Murray's place. His old barf-green Cadillac was parked in the driveway.

I hurried up to the fence and reached my arm over the top, feeling for the latch on the other side. My hand found it and pulled it up and I pushed the gate open. I saw a flickering orange glow illuminating the tall trees of the back yard and walked forward.

A ring of people in hooded vermilion robes stood around a large pyre. The full moon shone up above in the clear night. Embers floated up into the sky as I walked towards the fire, entranced. I saw my cat, sitting patiently in the circle, next to Mr. Murray. Her yellow eyes glowed in the light of the fire. Her fur was jet black except for a small square white patch at her throat. Her priest collar, as I had always thought of it.

The assembled ring of human forms turned and faced me in the dancing light of the fire. Their low rumbling chants were now silent. I looked ahead and to the right where movement and muffled screams caught my sudden attention. A burlap sack lay on the ground near a garden shed in the corner. The shape inside the bag which thrashed and kicked was clearly human, terrified, and drugged with almost enough of something, which appeared to be wearing off as their voice became gradually clearer and more desperate.

I stood there for what felt like a long time. Finally Mr. Murray spoke up.

"Well, Jason, is it?" he got my name wrong but under the circumstances I let it slide. "You appear to have caught us mid ceremony. Usually we.. err.. our rituals are more mundane. A goat or a fawn will usually appease Bahlrak. This week, however, his desires were greater. He requires a greater sacrifice every so often. When the moon is fat and full."

The assembled forms nodded, still staring at me. The screams grew louder and clearer from the burlap sack until someone walked over and pulled a hypodermic from their sleeve, injecting it quickly and wordlessly into the form in the bag.

"Ow! What the hell!?" the shape yelled from inside the bag, then slumped over and began to snore.

The hooded figure walked back and took its place in the circle again. They were all still staring at me, waiting for my answer to a question that was never asked.

"Okay, sure. Go Balrog! I'm in - sounds like fun." I hoped they would agree and decide to let me live, rather than making me a second superfluous sacrifice to their weird cat-god, a statue of which I now saw raised up on a pedestal closer to the house.

"BAHLRAK," the group said together simultaneously.

"Yeah, Ball-rack, sure. Man, you guys are great, getting together like this. It's good to have a social group, people with common interests.. um.." I was rambling. I stopped talking and waited for them to say something.

"If you wish to join us, you will be required to pass through initiation into the good grace of Bahlrak. One must be purified by fire." Mr. Murray spoke slowly, deliberately.

They held up their forearms, displaying brands melted into their flesh, portraying a dark horned symbol, which resembled a malevolent cat face. They waited with their arms held up, staring at me. Some of the brands appeared fresher than others and blood and pus appeared to ooze from the infected, putrefying flesh.

I realized if I did this and the wound became infected, a doctor would be out of the question. This was clearly a very secretive secret society. Which explained why they met at 3:30 AM in a back yard surrounded by large trees in a sparsely populated neighborhood. I took a deep breath and weighed the pros and cons. I decided to go along with it, rather than die by being burned alive.

I realized I had made the right decision when I nodded my head and Mr. Murray waved off the figure I had not noticed behind me, the one who had crept up slowly and quietly behind me with a syringe in its hand. I looked back, surprised, and the figure backed away into the shadows, its face invisible in the shadow of its hood.

"Welcome to the shadow society of Bahlrak, Jason." Mr. Murray was holding a brand in his tight grip now, though I hadn't seen him take it from the fire. Its tip glowed red in the darkness. His exposed wrist displayed its own brand. It appeared older and more fully healed than the others' in the group. I took it from this that he was the officiant of this dark and secret ceremony.

The others formed behind him and began to chant. They stared blankly as he approached, the glowing brand held up towards me.

Mr. Murray began to chant as well, and with his deep baritone added, it created a harmony effect, which was haunting and surprisingly beautiful.

I looked down and saw Peebs watching me closely, from within their midst, waiting to see what I would do.

I couldn't help but wonder what she was, really. Clearly not just a cat, I thought, but something else entirely.

As soon as that thought crossed my mind, her mouth formed into an evil grin. Have you ever seen a cat smile? Hope that you never do. It was the most terrifying thing I've ever seen. Her face wrinkled up beneath the eyes, showing sharp teeth glistening in the moonlight.

I screamed as the brand was pressed into my flesh. It melted my skin and I felt something hot dripping down my arm.

All I could see when I closed my eyes was that image of Peebs grinning. All teeth and shining yellow eyes…

So, my cat and I are in a bi-weekly social club now.

We meet Tuesdays and Thursdays, always at Mr. Murray's place, at 3:00 AM. Peebs comes too, of course. She's the dark priestess who silently officiates the ceremonies now. Mr. Murray has stepped down, as she is clearly the rightful leader of the group.

Bahlrak seems to be pleased, judging by how my backyard garden is doing this year. I was told the harvest would be bountiful after the sacrifice was given up as promised.

If you'd like to stop by one night, please do. Just be prepared to be judged by P.E. the Dark Priestess, Princess of Bahlrak.

Don't get off until the door is fully open

Mackenzie Elevator Repair is a low budget operation and most of the buildings that their repairmen like me are sent to are high-rise apartments in the poorer sections of town.

I was heading out to one such place, with my new trainee in tow.

He was fresh out of school and eager to impress. A bright young kid named Tommy – tall with short buzzed hair, always quick to smile and constantly joking around, but able to take things seriously when he had to. I was beginning to like him.

We got to the building and climbed out of our white service van with our duffel bag full of diagnostic gear.

Only a week before we had visited the place, to repair the same broken elevator. It was always on the fritz.

At least they had a back-up elevator, though, so we wouldn't have to climb the stairs   That was one of the worst parts of the job.   Some buildings had thirty flights of stairs and only one elevator – that was no longer working.

Those were not fun jobs to go to, since it would often mean climbing up and down the steps multiple times to reach the problem, and fetch the necessary parts and tools.

The superintendent met us in the lobby.

Immediately I couldn't help but notice a fat cockroach scurrying up the wall of the foyer. The place smelled like wet farts and flood damage that had never been repaired. There were yellow water stains on the ceiling and puddles on the aged vermilion carpet that we walked across towards the one working elevator.

"I don't know what the hell is wrong with this thing," the superintendent said.

I knew what was wrong with it. I had told him he needed to replace an expensive part but he was too cheap to fix it. As a result people were getting stuck in it constantly. That had happened to me in the same elevator not long before and I didn't envy anyone in that situation.

We stepped inside the other lift and I hit the button for the correct floor. I held down "close doors" and the "28" button at the same time. This would let us rise up to the top level without having to wait for people to get on and off. A little secret that firemen and repairmen alike use to get where we need to be a bit quicker.

The door closed with a squealing rattle as it dragged heavily across the threshold. It clanged shut with a loud metallic noise and we began to rise in the shaking box. It heaved back and forth as we ascended, knocking me off balance and into the wall. The old piece of shit was not improving with age.

"Is that normal?" Tommy asked.

"No."

We got to the top floor and the door opened up. Exiting the elevator, we heard the desperate calls for help from the box next to ours.

"HELP! It's so hot in here! I can't breathe! Please help us!"

"Hey, I'm the elevator repairman," I called down to them. "I'm here to get you out."

"Thank God!"

I heard the muffled sounds of their grateful voices as they spoke to each other. It sounded like there were a few of them. No wonder it was so hot in the tiny box.

The thought of all that body heat and packed people in such a crowded space filled me with sudden claustrophobic terror.

I had never been scared of confined spaces, until I got stuck in that very same box those people were trapped in. I remembered back to that day, sitting on the floor of the elevator, cockroaches scurrying around me everywhere in the dim, flickering light. The heat becoming oppressive and more overwhelming the longer I waited, the air becoming thick and humid and impossible to breathe. I can still remember it like it was yesterday...

Tommy and I tried to pry open the door and found it was completely jammed shut. Unusual to say the least, but not unheard of. It would require a trip downstairs to the van for a different tool. I let Tommy know what the plan was and the superintendent, Ronny, decided to come down as well, so that he could let us back in.

Down we went in the squealing elevator. It rattled and shook violently, descending to the lower levels.

We heard a *ding* and the door began to slide open, revealing the lobby. I had told Tommy a few rules before we started working together and as the elevator door slid across its steel track, he unthinkingly broke rule number three – "Don't get off the elevator while the door is still opening."

He began to exit as the door rattled open, and I began to say something, reaching out to grab his arm, but it was too late.

As he went through the threshold, the door suddenly slammed shut with tremendous speed and force. I would later find out that the superintendent had put this elevator out of service earlier that day, since it had almost decapitated someone else in a similar fashion.

No Sleep Tonight / Jordan Grupe

The superintendent didn't want to climb the stairs though, so when the other one was out of commission he just started using it again – but never mentioned it.

The old elevator's heavy steel door slid shut, slamming into Tommy with incredible force. Once it hit him it did not stop, but continued, crushing him like a sledgehammer through an overripe watermelon. Ever seen Gallagher? Yeah, kinda like that.

His nose caved in and his jaw shattered as the door crushed him with overwhelming power before I could intervene. He gurgled and spat out teeth as I rushed forward to try to push the door open. His head appeared partially caved in and I saw shards of his skull protruding from the flesh like broken pottery.

I was about to put my fingers in the gap but then thought better of it. Using the pry-bar instead, I tried to wrench it open. I jammed the edge of it into the doorframe, just above Tommy's head.

That was when the elevator began to suddenly ascend again, this time much quicker.

Tommy was still partially trapped, half in and half out the door, with the entire thing slammed through the middle of him. The pry-bar, and then the top of the elevator door came down on his head as we rose up to the next floor, caving his skull in from a different direction. That was all his brutalized body could take, and the left side of him collapsed into the lift. The other half was still outside, in the lobby, and we left it behind as we went up.

I began to scream with terror at what had happened, but the superintendent didn't seem fazed. He just looked at me calmly as the box rattled and went up with increasing speed.

"Shit," he said. "That's not good. Hey, can you keep a secret? I've got cash. We can tell people he was screwing around and got caught in the door. Nobody's fault. Or I can tell them you shoved him. It's up to you."

He smiled with his greasy grin. A thick gold chain necklace hung around his sweaty neck and his bald head gleamed with beads of perspiration as he waited for my response.

Before I could say anything, we began to freefall. The box dropped as if the cable had been cut, and I felt my stomach lurch and the cheeseburger I had eaten for lunch began to rise up into my throat in sudden protest.

If we'd been on the top floor we'd have died for sure, but we hadn't gotten that far up yet. Still, the impact was deafening, and the force of us stopping suddenly rattled my bones with horrifying pain.

Ronny, the superintendent, had been brought down to the floor with sudden force, and I saw his forehead was bleeding. He was missing a couple teeth as well.

We began to ascend again, and my heart was hammering fast in my chest. I wanted to get off this hellish ride.

Suddenly it stopped.

I heard another *ding* and the elevator door opened in the lobby, revealing the other half of Tommy, as well as a small crowd of disgusted and curious tenants.

The super got up, scrambling to his feet, and tried to dive out of the box. He didn't quite make it.

The door stopped moving and slammed shut once again, landing with sickening force against his bloated midsection. I heard several ribs cracking loudly and he screamed as it drove itself into him. Blood poured from his mouth and I raced over to the controls and hit the "door open" button.

Nothing happened.

With a large spray of blood like a beach ball sized water balloon exploding, his body was torn completely in half by the door.

I hit the button again and it opened. I waited patiently for it to slide all the way across the track and reach the other side. Then and only then did I step forward with confidence, leaving the gore-filled elevator behind.

There was going to be a ton of paperwork after all this, I thought. Too bad, I had liked the kid. But you gotta remember the rules. Maybe I should move that one up the list.

No Sleep Tonight / Jordan Grupe

International Ghoul-Hunters: Operation Roundtable
General Reed's Worst Day

At first, when the dead began to rise, there was panic.
Mayhem.   Everything we had seen in movies and
television. It all came to pass.

All governments were wiped out   Every world leader
killed and reanimated. The systems and structures that
we had all come to rely on were revealed for the thin
and fragile glass towers that they were – and they
shattered into a million pieces. It was total anarchy.
At least for a little while.

Small groups of survivors such as myself roamed the
countryside for months, looking for shelter, setting up
camps.   That was how it started in the beginning.
Hunter-gatherer types, we travelled around trying to
find a place to call home for a little while, until the
hordes began to form and cluster together, wiping out
everything in their path. Then we'd move on.

But after a while, structures began to form. Systems.
Organization from the chaos.   Evenness from the
entropy.

I was within that elite group of disciplined warrior
survivors from the very beginning, those of us who
decided to make change for the better, and to set up
something to replace the nothing that currently existed.

That was how I.G.O.R. was formed. International Ghoul-Hunters: Operation Roundtable.

By that point we had a few pilots who could take us around and bring us all together for face-to-face meetings when we had to. We had also managed to set up a rudimentary Internet again, that we could all use for the purposes of communication. It wasn't anywhere near as good as the original, of course. More akin to a BBS platform from the 1990s. But it was something.

The Roundtable, as we called it at first, was a loose organization of leaders from various nations who wanted to work collaboratively together to bring the world back to normal. And to deal with *The Superiors*

The Superiors were what we called the zombies who had started to evolve. They terrified all of us more than anything we had ever seen, and we knew if we didn't take them out they would destroy us all. Every bit of progress we had made would be undone.

Of course, every roundtable needs an Arthur, and we had one. Perhaps that was the reason why we named the organization what we did. I honestly don't remember. But it was he who brought us all together.

Who knows if that was his real name or not. But it was all I ever knew him as. Of course he was British to boot. I'm Canadian, myself. We had Americans as well, along with Germans, French, Brazilians, Koreans,

Australians, Africans, and representatives from a dozen other countries. It was a big table.

Arthur had agents planted all over the world, and I was one of them. We rooted out The Superiors and reported back to him with our findings. Then he would send backup as necessary to take them out before they could build too big of an army.

Oh yeah, did I mention The Superiors could telekinetically control entire hordes of zombies? Because that's the whole problem with them. You can't have people like that around in the zombie apocalypse. You just can't. It's not a good idea to let folks like that hang around. They're nothing but trouble.

The guy I'm about to tell you about was no exception.

It was a typical reconnaissance mission at first. We were in the downtown core of Toronto, the burnt-out husks of towering buildings all around us. The city of a couple million people was a hollow shell of its former self.

No one would have dared go into the city at the beginning. But now it was a different story. The undead ghouls who had taken over were few and far between after years of hard times. And we could take care of them handily. At least, so we thought.

"Want to check out the old Rogers Center?" someone asked. I think it might have been Cassie. Or then again it could have been Stella. It doesn't matter. It was no one's fault.

"Sure," I said. If it had been a busier day I'd have said no. I was the leader after all. But it was quiet. We had barely run into any undead since that morning. It was like they were all hiding out somewhere.

"I miss going to see the Blue Jays. Even if they never did win another one without Joe Carter."

We walked up the long staircase off of Front Street, making our way towards the stadium. I had an image in my mind of going out onto the field, picking up a bat, and hitting a ball with it. I imagined it sailing into the outfield, a major league home run. Usually I was so mission-focused. But I was goofing off that day. Maybe I was just tired of the grind. I think maybe it was something else, though.

The glass doors were all smashed out, making it easy to get inside. There were a couple zombies milling around the foyer, and we made quick work of them. Cassie drove her katana blade through an eyeball, Frank caved in a skull with his sledgehammer.

The security gates had been destroyed by looters and we slipped past them easily. We made our way towards the playing field and I was overwhelmed by nostalgia. Memories of going to see baseball games with my wife, my family, my friends. It all came flooding back.

My knees buckled from the emotion of it all. They were dead. Every last one of them. I would never see any of them ever again. I would never watch a baseball game ever again.

What was the point of it all?

My team must have sensed my sudden melancholy because they stopped with me and actually said a few sympathetic words.

"Hey man, you okay?" Frank asked.

"Give him a minute. He's dealing with something. We've all got shit from our past that comes back sometimes."

I shook my head, trying to get rid of the thoughts. It wasn't easy.

"Let's go play some ball," I said, trying to smile and feeling it stretch fake across my face.

Frank wasn't buying it, but was nice enough not to say anything. He put his meaty arm around me and the five of us went down the aisle towards the playing field. Tom was quiet as usual, keeping an eye out behind us for anyone looking to sneak up on us.

Surprisingly enough, the dugout still contained a few baseball bats and balls. Even a couple of gloves. We went out onto the field, and I saw the nervous looks on everyone's faces. It had been so quiet lately, but we knew how fast things could change. Still, we thought we could handle anything.

Frank threw a pitch at the strike zone. It was a lob and I managed to give it a good crack on the first swing. The ball went sailing into the air and towards left field. Cassie ran for it and grabbed it, throwing it back into the infield. Stella was playing catcher behind home plate, while Tom stood off to the side of the field in the stands, looking around, waiting for trouble.

"Come on, Tom," I yelled. "It's no fun without another batter. If you come down you can take a swing next."

I thought he would say no. Tom was always the one who stayed off to the side while the rest of us had these brief moments of fun. The stoic bastard never wanted any part of it. But he surprised me and he came down to the field, actually grinning for once. I handed him the bat and he stood at the plate, waiting for the next pitch.

The huge empty major league baseball stadium was hauntingly quiet, our every movement echoing across the vast space around us.

Frank threw the ball a couple more times before Tom managed to get a hit. The ball went far into center field and Cassie went running for it.

Tom made a dash for first base, then for second. Frank was out there yelling for Cassie to throw it into him at second, saying they would get him out there.

That was when I saw them. I was speechless for a minute, and the ball almost hit me in the head when someone threw it into home plate after an error. They had all been focused on the play and didn't see what was happening all around us.

At all of the entrances, all around the field, undead were filtering in like patrons just before a big game was about to start. They were coming down the aisles toward us from every direction.

It took a minute for the others to notice. I was too dumbstruck to say anything.

Our game stopped entirely when they saw me looking and noticed our dilemma. Everyone dropped their baseball mitts and ran for their weapons. But we knew it was hopeless. We knew we were doomed. There was clearly a Superior here, in the stadium with us. He was commanding the undead that were surrounding us on all sides. That was the only way they could be so organized.

They wandered onto the field lazily, without haste, only revealing their surprising hunger as they came close enough to smell our warmth and our sweat. Then they appeared suddenly ravenous, opening their mouths wide and snapping at us with unnatural speed.

The ghouls went after poor Frank the worst. He was a huge man, about 6ft 10. The Superior probably saw him and commanded them to go after him first.

He swung his sledgehammer around in a giant arc, obliterating several zombies' heads with one fell swoop. But there was a wolf among them.

Wolves are what we call the fast ones. The ones who act slow at first but then attack with stunning speed and ingenuity. They're not Superiors, but they're close. Ever hear the expression, "Like a wolf in sheep's clothing"? That's why we call them that. Because you think they're normal ghouls, but then they surprise you and tear your throat out with their bare hands.

The wolf jumped on Frank while his back was turned, swinging his hammer in a great arc around him.

It landed on his back and began to tear at the muscles of his neck, ripping them apart while he screamed.

As I was distracted by that, four zombies surrounded me and I had to sidestep quickly to prevent myself from getting devoured. I quickly swung the black bat I was carrying and caught one upside the head, causing him to stagger backwards. He regained his balance almost instantly and came towards me again.

While I was momentarily focused on that, the other three came at me, as well as six more. We were quickly becoming outnumbered. And hundreds more were swarming in by the second.

They were storming the field like an angry mob. Only this mob was intent on eating our flesh.

The smell of them all was horrifying, and the terror I felt overwhelming. All I could see were rotten faces all around me, black teeth and eyeballs oozing pus. Their skin was grey and decaying, with gaps and tears showing exposed muscle and bone beneath.

And the noise of them all! Moaning and gurgling while they attacked us with a complete lack of emotion or awareness.

I saw Cassie go down and her sword went flying into the air and landed near me. Hurrying over to it, I picked it up off the ground. Knowing how much it meant to her, I wanted to keep it safe. Even if it was only as a tribute to her.

Her terrified and desperate screams rang out hollow across the field.

That was when I vowed that I would get out of there, one way or another.

The wolf-zombie came running towards me and launched itself into the air. I drove the sword's point into his eye as he did and the momentum carried his head right through the steel, destroying his brain.

At that moment I realized all of my friends were dead. The horde was zeroing in on me, with no one else to focus their efforts on.

Big Frank "The Tank" stood tall among them, his eyes now red and full of hunger and hate.

No Sleep Tonight / Jordan Grupe

Cassie stood up next, and stalked towards me, joining the crowd of undead as they approached.

They attacked me without mercy, my friends and foes alike. As if we had never known each other. I fought like I had never fought before. And let me tell you, I'm known for my ability to get out of situations even as completely fucked up as this one was.

I slashed off zombie faces with the katana, cutting heads off while spinning like a dervish and somersaulting through the air. I parried and thrusted, hacked and slashed, dove through legs and climbed atop the crowd's shoulders, severing heads and bouncing upon the ones that stood there, jam-packed together, using them as planks to springboard to and fro from while I did my dirty work.

Eventually the pile of corpses was staggeringly high. It filled the baseball field almost.

But even I have my limits. My arms were filled with blood, heavy and clumsy, after hours of defending myself from a never-ending onslaught of undead.

One of them was cunning, and quick. A wolf, probably. I thought I had them all beat, but he grabbed me and took me down. And that was it. I was finished, I assumed, as the crowd of those remaining came at me and descended upon me with salivating mouths and hungry eyes, their teeth bared and hands outstretched like greedy infants reaching for a teat.

But the Superior had other plans.

He floated in on the air itself, descending among the crowd of them just as they were about to consume my flesh.

"You, I will keep alive," he said. "You are strong. And I like strong people by my side. I will keep you as my scribe. You will write what will become the new history books, telling of my conquests. Making it known for generations after, that it was I who created this new world!"

"Uhh.. Thanks?" I wasn't really happy with the new arrangement he was imposing. But then again I wasn't really in a position to argue.

"Does that mean they aren't going to eat my brains?"

"Precisely! We can't have the new scribe stumbling around, drooling all over the scrolls as he writes the history books, can we?"

I was very relieved. He noticed that and made a little tsk noise.

"Oh, I didn't mean for you to get too excited. I said they can't eat your brains. I didn't say anything about the rest of you!"

The undead looked at me with hungry eyes once again, now having obtained permission to enjoy a meal. Albeit within a limited menu.

No Sleep Tonight / Jordan Grupe

"Only his lower extremities, please! He'll need those hands of his to write with! We wouldn't want that juicy brain to go to waste, now would we?"

The pack of them closest to me began to pull strips of flesh off of my body with their bare hands as I screamed. They drooled and slobbered as they feasted on my legs and feet, until there was nothing left of them.

The pain was unimaginable. The suffering... well, it's pointless to talk about that now...

I have a new kind of suffering to deal with at this point in my life.

Now I get to write about the new world as it is created. A horror play land for a demented psychopath who enjoys nothing more than torment and suffering. He controls them all now. The whole lot of them.

I get dragged around like his publicist, putting out press releases that nobody can read but me and him. And I'm starting to get the feeling he's practically illiterate.

I sure hope I.G.O.R. is still out there, somewhere. If not, I'm really fucked.

International Ghoul-Hunters: Operation Roundtable
A Tale from the Tower

International Ghoul-hunters: Operation Roundtable was a long-winded name for our attempt to restructure society after its collapse. We shortened it to IGOR, and have referred to it as such ever since.

The zombie apocalypse happened nearly a decade ago, and I'm old enough to remember the shock and ensuing mayhem experienced by the general populace when we saw that TV shows and movies had gotten it right all along. "Go for the head" was the word that got out. That was the only way to kill the bastards. Destroy the brain. Or at least what was left of it.

Methods of infection were disputed at first, some saying even being touched by a zombie was enough to become infected by the virus. Some thought it was airborne. Others believed it was only spread through a bite.

People who died of natural causes stayed dead, at least. The only ones who rose again were the people who were bit by a ghoul, we realized after some time. There didn't seem to be any chance of infection through scratches or aerosols, which was a relief. That meant we had a chance of getting things back under control one day, if we could only thin out their numbers.

IGOR came into being a few years ago, and has grown tremendously since then. We have a good chance now at taking back the world for humanity, and snatching it back from the grasp of the dead. An attempt at global government that had enough local clout and manpower to affect change across the planet. We created a global communication network, and even have a small navy and air force. It's not much, but it's a start. And like I say, we keep growing every day.

The problem, though, is the superiors. If it weren't for them we'd have the world back to normal, almost. But the superiors are dangerous and deadly. Able to control entire hordes of zombies telepathically. And they've been taking out our people one by one. Systematically destroying our new shadow government and replacing it with their own.

One superior in particular has amassed a huge army of undead. We've come to calling him Lucifer, as he's risen to the heights of evil power unlike anything we've seen before. He is like the antichrist. Raising up an army of dead to replace the living.

He started out in Northern Ontario, Canada. The cold weather froze many of the zombies in the winter months, keeping them fresher, stronger.

Somehow, he amassed the largest horde ever seen from what was left in the colder regions and then began to move south towards Toronto, where he set up his headquarters. Right at the top of the CN tower.

For those who don't know, that was once the tallest building in the world. It's still near the top of the record books, especially after several of its competitors burned down following the looting and rioting post-apocalypse.

Lucifer lives at the top of this giant tower, and rules supreme over the hundreds of thousands of undead who roam the streets below him. From up there, he can survey them all, and send them forth against any threats that approach, using only his thoughts.

Our man is still inside, so we don't want to blow the place up. We think he knows that. Maybe that's why he's keeping him there. The rest of the team is dead – Frank, Cassie, Stella, Tom – he only kept the leader.

General Reed. My once-proud mentor. Now a tortured captive, only half the man he used to be. Literally, not figuratively, since the zombies ate his legs. Mentally he's all there – we can tell this based on his writings. He's not reporting to us directly, but it seems he's still managing to sneak out the occasional hidden code within his writings.

It appears that Lucifer has made General Reed into his publicist. The guy was always a great writer. He did our meeting minutes and whenever we needed a memo for some big-picture idea typed up he was always the one we asked to do it. So it doesn't surprise me that Lucifer enlisted him to write up these press releases for no discernable reason, which he leaves scattered everywhere.

Here's a brief excerpt from one:

"Greetings!

All hail our supreme leader! The nameless one. He will carry us forth into the future with his brave and fierce lamentations. Make way for his greatness! Pffft.. yeah, okay.

What else is new?

Today's groan of the day is: "UNNNNGGGGHHHH"

And here's a joke to brighten up this cloudy morning!

Did you hear about the guy who's addicted to drinking brake fluid? He says he can stop anytime he wants!"

You get the basic idea. Just a community newsletter more or less, except nobody can read it but us and him. And I don't mean Lucifer. Judging by his lack of awareness that he is being openly mocked in the majority of these press releases, I would say he has a cursory understanding of the English language at best.

Which brings me to how we ended up being tipped off on when and where to strike. In one particular press release, General Reed filled us in on the fact that Lucifer really likes to sleep in on Sundays. He always stays up late the night before, for Decapitated Head Bowling League – every Tuesday and Saturday night.

Thus we had our opening for an attack.

The plan was to come in by chopper and descend to the observation deck of the CN tower. We would have to blast our way in, then rappel inside. It was the only way, since there was a few hundred thousand zombies downstairs.

Hovering over the tall building, we dropped down from the helicopters on our ropes. I only hoped the sound of the rotor blades hadn't woken the bastard up.

Controlling my descent, I slowly dropped down to the window on the south side of the building. The observation deck had a ledge on the exterior, so I was able to stand on that easily and get prepared.

I gave the hand signal to Reggie on my left, then to Sam on my right. We placed the explosive charges on the plexi-glass, knowing it was thick and wouldn't break easily.

My thumb went up into the air to indicate I was ready, and they pulled me back up towards the chopper.

Once we were clear of the blast, I hit the detonation button.

The explosion was deafening, despite my attempts to cover my ears with my hands at the last second. The intended effect was achieved, though, and we saw movement inside the building. We had made our way in, but now they knew we were coming. I gave the hand signal to the team and we dropped down once again from our safe height near the choppers.

As the roller clamp slid down and I got closer and closer to the building's observation deck once again, my heart began to hammer wildly in my chest. Despite my efforts at controlling it, I knew I might die there. We had never faced anyone so unpredictable. So deadly.

My feet hit the steel grate floor of the observation deck and I saw zombies milling about inside the building. We just had to hope that he hadn't made it to the elevator yet. The blueprints showed it was not far from where he slept.

I jumped through the open window and felt the air whipping around inside the place with tremendous force. It was a windy night and at this height the gales were powerful enough to knock a man off his feet.

A zombie lurched out of the shadows towards me and I spun around just in time. It was a fast one, a wolf.

I managed to knock his chin with the butt of my rifle but it did very little to disable the monster. His rotten teeth snapped the open air just inches from my face. His decaying skin had large sections missing which exposed muscle, bone, and subcutaneous tissue beneath. I could see his jaw snapping shut through a large hole in his cheek.

Reggie came up behind him as the bastard took me to the ground with his wild and unpredictable attacks.
We all try to watch each other's backs, and Reggie was a consummate professional.

He made quick work of the wolf with a thrust of his long tactical knife through the brain stem of the ghoul.

General Reed began to call out from his location. We heard him and moved in that direction. Lucifer would conceivably want to use him as a human shield, so it was a safe bet they would be together. Either that or the bastard was already gone. We didn't think he would leave without his scribe and bargaining chip.

Without General Reed as a deterrent, we'd have napalmed his ass long ago. A few suggested doing that regardless, but were outvoted by the rest of the roundtable. Arthur wouldn't have allowed it anyway, and he had the ultimate say with his veto power.

Broken glass crunched beneath my feet as I moved towards the sound of Reed's calls for help. The man sounded much different now, like he was weak and in ill-health. His strong voice now sounded tired and haggard.

"Look out!" I heard Miller call out too late, and turned to see Reggie being assaulted from all angles. The floor was full of wolf-zombies, I realized too late. They were Lucifer's elite bodyguards. These mutated ghouls were capable of inhuman speed and their reflexes were off the charts. Worse yet, they were sneaky. They could blend into the shadows and lie in wait for hours or days if they wanted to. Not to mention their ability to mimic normal dullard zombie behaviour, so you didn't realize you were dealing with a wolf until it was too late, and they were already pulling out your windpipe with their teeth.

Reggie was currently having that done to him. They pulled out his trachea and esophagus and gnawed on them as he gurgled and made silent screams.

I took out my sidearm and shot one in the head. The other looked up at me with his face covered in gore, and he smiled intelligently. The next bullet took out his eye and he fell over, dead for good.

Suddenly all the shadowy corners inside the CN tower observation deck looked like potential hiding places for ghouls. They were anywhere and everywhere, as far as we could tell. I made a hand signal to the other members of the team, and we made a tight formation, watching each other's backs.

We began to move towards the direction of General Reed once again. His calls for help were silent now, and I worried we had missed our chance. For all we knew they had snuck onto the elevator and were now down on the ground floor, escaping.

I kicked in the door to the room where I believed his calls had come from. It was clearly not the right room. Ghouls were packed inside shoulder to shoulder, filling the crowded room with a horrifying smell. As soon as they saw me they lunged forward, reaching out their decaying hands toward me. I screamed and stumbled backwards, as they began to pour out of the room. There was no chance of containing them. They were soon everywhere.

I began to fire my assault rifle, taking measured single shots, trying to remember my training, trying not to panic. It helped that I had been in the shit before. Worse than this, if you can imagine that.

But there were dozens of them. They quickly overwhelmed my team and took them out one by one, despite their efforts to fight back. Pretty soon it was just me and a handful of zombies, lurching towards me as I picked them off with careful shots to the head.

When the last one hit the ground, I figured it was time to try another door. There were only so many options. General Reed had to be behind one of them. But Lucifer was probably hiding in there too. I hadn't heard the elevator door opening, I realized, which meant that he was most likely still up here.

The next door I kicked in was the right one. I saw General Reed laying on the floor, a cold look in his eyes. His lower half was gone, and the rest of him looked thin and pale. He was shaking his head and looking at me saying, "Why did you come here? You shouldn't have come here."

I stepped into the room and his eyes widened. Turning around, I saw the blade of a long sword swish past my face. It took off the end of my nose but I didn't feel that until later. The adrenaline took over as Lucifer regained his balance and began to take a backswing with the blade. It looked heavy and ornate, and completely impractical.

When he swung it, it threw him off balance once again, and I took my opportunity as I sidestepped out of the path of danger. He howled with rage and anger as I took hold of the hilt of the sword, attempting to wrestle it from his grasp. He was strong, but I was stronger, and began to overpower him.

That was when he bit me. It was a move made out of pure desperation, and I could tell by the look on his face that he was afraid of what the consequences of this action might be.

No one had ever been bit by a superior before. Until that moment.

I felt the power surging through me and although I didn't understand it at the time, my life in that moment would be changed forever.

I kicked him away from me as I pulled the blade out of his hands. The flesh of my neck where his teeth were tearing it apart came loose and I swore in anger and horrified pain. The blood which poured forth from the wound was now black and tarry, and didn't look like something which would come from a human being. I realized that was because I no longer was one. Now I was something different. Now I was a superior. My heart was no longer beating, I noticed. My skin felt cold and clammy.

The elevator made a loud ding, and I heard the door open just outside the room we were in. I gave the superior another good kick to the chest and shoved him out the door just as a dozen more zombies came around the corner.

"Eat him!" I shouted at them, wanting to test my new powers.

They engulfed him and began to tear apart his clothing and then his flesh as he screamed and howled in pain and terror.

"Go out the window! Take him with you!" I shouted at them next. My new undead servants complied, and took the bastard down to the ground floor with them, pulling him out the window as he screamed in bloody agony. Lucifer was no more. By the time they hit the ground they would all be liquefied human remains. Zombie smoothies.

"What's your status team leader?" the voice of the helicopter pilot demanded through my radio.

"Package is in hand," I said back, clipping a rope to General Reed's belt.

"Thank you," he said weakly.

"Don't thank me until we're home free, okay? You'll jinx this flawless mission which has gone off without a hitch. So just keep your trap shut for now, alright?"

I threw him over my shoulder and carried him to the window, stepping out onto the observation deck. From there, I made the call with the radio. We were going home. And now we had a chance at fighting back.

No Sleep Tonight / Jordan Grupe

Added Bonus: A taste of Jordan's Next Book:

Editor's Note: This concludes *No Sleep Tonight* – we hope you've enjoyed this remarkable collection of short stories. As an added bonus, we are now sharing an excerpt from Jordan Grupe's latest upcoming novel *The Go-Between Tree*...

Prologue

Once upon a time, not so long ago, there was a town called Hollow's End. In this little town there was a forest. And within this forest grew a tree.

The tree – known as the Go-Between tree in other worlds but not our own – was hidden in plain sight, unknown to the people of earth, who seldom visited the forests anymore. They had no idea of its potential. Of its incredible power and the tunnels that could be opened up from within it.

The Go-Between tree looked much like any other old oak tree. It was quite tall, and one would guess it was a few centuries old at least. People didn't realize that the tree was actually as old as time itself, and could take you places that you would have never known existed. Mirror images of our world, millions upon millions of them, some very different from ours, others identical except for a few small changes.

Perhaps it was the power of the tree that made Hollow's End such a strange and magical place.

There seemed to be no other reason for it. On the surface there was nothing unusual, of course. To a tourist or passerby they would have no idea. But for those who lived there, the mystical qualities of the town were undeniable.

No one knew about the Go-Between tree from our world. Then, many years ago, a man stumbled across it – quite literally, in fact – tripping over its roots which blended in perfectly with the autumn leaves on the ground.

For whatever reason, the tree was perhaps lonely that day, it opened up to him. Maybe it saw some good in him, but if it did that goodness is long gone.

After that the tree lay dormant and forsaken, looking very much like a regular old oak once again for a long, long time, until recently.

On a day not too long ago, when it opened up again. From the dark space beneath its sturdy trunk and ancient roots, a man's fingers appeared. Then his hands and forearms as he pulled himself up with a great effort. He looked old and weathered as the wood of the ancient oak.

He carried with him a large, ornately carved trunk. A war chest. The man went into some nearby shrubbery and disappeared for a minute, then emerged by himself, the chest left behind, hidden in the overgrowth. He looked around the woods and took a deep breath in. He scowled at the smell, wrinkling his nose, and trudged away.

Part One

1   *One year later...*

The noise of the automated pill crusher was loud.

Not loud enough to drown out the call bells though, Jerome thought to himself as he poured the packet of ground-up medication into a little cup of applesauce and swirled it around with a spoon.   He mixed it together into a disgusting-looking brown and yellow paste. *Stool softeners and Sinemet, what a breakfast.*

An urgent chime began, replacing the soft ringing of the call bells, indicating someone had ripped the cord right out of the wall.   Usually such an aggressive action was only reserved for emergencies – at least in theory – in reality confused patients and careless cleaners pulled the cords out of the walls all the time.   He waited for the sound to stop once the person in the room noticed their mistake.   He could have sworn he had seen Becky go in there a few minutes before.

Jerome looked down the hall and saw the light was still flashing double-time.   It should have gone off by now.

All of the staff members on the floor were in other rooms, getting the residents dressed and transferring them to their wheelchairs for the day.   It wasn't uncommon for the call bells to be left unanswered for long stretches, unfortunately.   But the sound of this particular one was causing a sinking feeling inside of Jerome that he didn't like very much.

He went back to what he was doing and then was surprised when a visitor walked briskly past him, wearing a coat and baseball cap, pulled low over his face. A resident's son, leaving after a brief visit, he figured. It was pretty early in the day for someone to come in, but not unheard of.

The man proceeded to the double doors of the unit. He pushed but they wouldn't open. Stepping back, he looked around, then saw the keypad to his left. Scratching his head, he walked over to it and hovered his fingers over the buttons for a few moments, as if trying to remember the code.

"It's 9-5-0-2!" Jerome shouted across the hallway to him. They were about twenty yards away from each other, but he thought the man looked vaguely familiar. He had a large ring on his finger with a big, polished black stone set into it.

"Thanks," the man replied, his gravelly, accented voice familiar. *Who is he?* Jerome wondered. He knew him from somewhere. The hair rose up on the back of Jerome's neck and goose-bumps rose on his skin, but he couldn't discern what was causing these sensations.

The call bell continued to wail, like a hungry infant.

Sighing resignedly, he put the cup of gritty brown and yellow applesauce into the drawer marked 104, to return to it later. Jerome closed the medication tab for this room on the computer and scrolled down to the other one marked 114 – Varduin, Yeltzik.

Jerome knew he was going to have to go down there. Might as well see if the old guy was due for any meds while he was in there turning off the bell. Maybe Becky needed a second person to supervise while she transferred Yeltzik to his wheelchair. She shouldn't be there alone by herself, really. The guy had a history of "behaviours" as they like to call them nowadays. But then again, it seemed like they *all* had *behaviours*.

Clicking through the various tabs, Jerome finally reached the one for Yeltzik in room 114. His eyes widened in panic as he realized a few of the tabs were coloured red, indicating medications had been missed. Jerome had just begun his shift an hour before, but the night nurse was assigned from an agency and they were sometimes flaky. Surely she'd been told about Yeltzik and his past when she got the report from the evening nurse? Was that nurse Marcy? She wasn't the most thorough, especially on Friday nights when she was anxious to go to the club with friends after work.

He clicked through and saw that none of the anti-psychotics had been given. None of the hypnotics or tranquilizers or sedatives. His hands trembling, he grabbed a vial of Haldol and drew up much more than was prescribed.

"Olga, Sheila, Brenda! I need your help, right now!" He shouted from the med cart. Some of the more mobile and independent residents popped their heads out of their rooms to see what was happening and what the commotion was all about.

He twisted off the blunt-tipped needle he'd used to draw up the medication and exchanged it for a freshly wrapped IM needle, which was long, sharp, and wide-bore. The other stuff, the stronger medication, was held in a locked cabinet, and there was no time for that right now. He would have someone fetch that for him later – rules be damned.

The bell was still wailing quickly, louder and louder it seemed to him – no longer sounding like an infant dying of hunger, but like a police siren, an ambulance. The other staff members came out to join him in the hallway, looking confused and anxious.

"Yeltzik didn't get his medication this morning," Jerome said to them. Their eyes went wide and Olga actually gasped out loud. *Good*, he thought, *they understood what that meant.*

"Becky is in there," Brenda said. "I told her I was going to meet her in a minute to help get him up to his chair."

"No one is ever supposed to go in there alone, didn't you tell her that?" Jerome was growing angry now, already seeing by the look on her face that the answer was no, none of them had told her. She probably had no idea what that man was capable of. It was only her second day on the job, her first day on this particular unit.

"I meant to -" Brenda tried to say but he cut her off before she could finish.

"Move!" Jerome shoved past her and motioned for them to follow him as they made their way down the hallway past the surprised faces of residents in their doorways.

"Can you shut off that damn buzzing!?" One of the residents called out in a strained, shrill voice from her room. He ignored this and went past as she protested.

The door to the room was closed, he saw, pushing it open and entering 114. He felt a cool breeze coming in and thought it strange, since the windows in the rooms didn't open in the locked unit.

Jerome saw the window was broken and blood and glass were on it and everywhere – the floors, walls, ceiling.

Worst of all, young Becky was lying on the ground, her pretty bespectacled face in ruins. Blood was soaked into her hair and a puddle of it was spreading around her skull. A gash was torn across her scalp and he looked closer to see it went very deep, exposing shattered bone flaked throughout the grey matter beneath. Her white-knuckled fist was clutching the call bell, which had been ripped out of the wall.

Becky gurgled and breathed in shallow, bubbling breaths as he walked in slowly, unsure of what to do next. Things came to him after a few moments of silent panic and he began to speak.

"Brenda, call the police. Tell them Yeltzik Verduin has escaped. Tell them to send an ambulance, and to hurry. Life threatening bleeding and a very bad head injury - tell them that." Jerome went over to Becky's body and listened to her breathing with his stethoscope. Crackles and wheezes echoed back through the earpieces. Blood in her lungs.

Jerome saw it now on her dark scrub top as well. A pool spreading around several stab wounds in her abdomen and chest. She began to cough and specks of blood sprayed into the air and spread mist-like around them.

Brenda had hurried out of the room and Olga was asking what she could do to help. Sheila was slowly backing away, looking terrified and trembling. He realized he couldn't rely on her for assistance.

"Go to the med room and get all the gauze you see in there and bring it back here!" Olga began to leave the room and he called after her as an afterthought, "AND VASELINE!"

She came back a couple minutes later and he applied the bandages to Becky's wounds. The Vaseline-soaked ones he put on the wounds that bubbled and appeared to lead into her lungs. This would keep a temporary seal and help her to breathe a bit easier until the paramedics could get her to the hospital and insert a chest tube.

With Becky temporarily stabilized, breathing in regular, shallow breaths, Jerome looked at the broken window again. He was definitely going to be fired.

2

Phoebe was having a quiet day, browsing google news in between calls, when an alert sounded and a message popped up on her computer screen indicating someone had dialled 9-1-1.

She made note of the location and phone number of the caller. Pleasant Woods Long Term Care Facility.

Uh oh, thought Phoebe, *another ambulance trip to the hospital for some geezer who tripped and broke their hip, or worse, a stroke or MI,* those happened sometimes too. Pneumonia was another one, but less common this time of year, towards the end of August, before the start of cold and flu season.

"9-1-1, what's your emergency?" She said in a practiced, clear voice.

"We need an ambulance! One of the PSWs was attacked by a patient! And the police, too. He broke the window and ran away. Life threatening bleeding! Head injury!"

That was a new one.

The woman was barely understandable in her panic. She was in shock, Phoebe had heard the same thing a hundred times, a thousand, even.

"Okay, listen to me. What's your name?" This tactic usually worked best. People enjoyed the sound of their own name. It soothed them.

"Brenda." The woman's voice was slightly calmer now. *Good.*

"Brenda, I need you to listen to me very closely. Try to answer as best you can. Will you do that for me?" She had already taken the simple steps to send police and ambulance to the scene, now it was time to do some preliminary investigation, as she was trained to do. Whatever was said from the moment the woman began the call until the she hung up could be used in court, in case an investigation was launched into the home. It had happened before. But Brenda didn't need to know all that.

"Yes, of course, whatever I can do to help," she said.

3

"Jayson! Turn off the game and get your butt over here!" Tammy hated to yell but that was the third time she had asked.

"Just a sec," Jayson turned off the Nintendo Switch and his Zelda game went to sleep.

"What time are you going to be back for dinner?" She asked as they both put their shoes on by the front door.

"Is five-thirty okay?"

"That's fine, but don't make it any later than that. I'm making tacos, by the way, your favourite."

"Yeah tacos are alright, I guess "

Perfect, thought Tammy. Last week he wanted tacos every night for the rest of his life, now they're 'alright'. She loved the kid, but he was such a picky eater sometimes. By this time next month he would tell her he hated tacos and didn't want to look at them ever again.

"Okay, I'll see you at five-thirty, no later!" She kissed him on the cheek and gave him a hug, then locked the door and they went their separate ways. Jayson jumped on his bike and she watched him ride off. At least he was wearing a helmet this time, although she had no doubt he would take it off and stuff it into his backpack once he was around the corner. Cool kids don't wear helmets, of course. Traumatic brain injuries are all the rage these days, after all.

She sighed and got into her little economy car and backed out of the driveway…

Editor's Note: This concludes the additional free bonus excerpt from Jordan Grupe's upcoming novel *The Go-between Tree* - be sure to look for it online on Amazon sites worldwide and at other online retailers and better bookstores everywhere.

Manor House
www.manor-house-publishing.com